# TALES
## OF THE
# GOLDEN PATH

# BY KING ERIC I

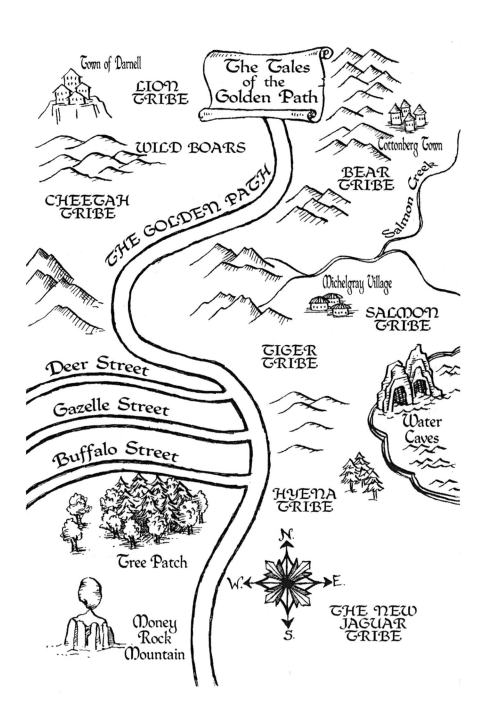

# INTRODUCTION

In a world similar to ours there is a Golden Path. Its land provides sustenance for all who live upon it, but not all live there. Jealousy, ambition and greed attract invaders and foster enemies, both foreign and domestic.

Intrigue, betrayal, destiny, respect and royalty are in play, bringing to light the consequences of what many had thought, and some had hoped, were simply faded tales from The Golden Path's history.

# DEDICATION

This book was a long time coming, and I could not have done it without God and every one of you.

My mother, Brenda Nelson Patrick. My father, Matthew Gardner, and his wife, Marie. My two beautiful grandmothers, Ola Mae Murray and Nevada Majors.

My dear sister, Angel Patrick. You went through it all with me. To my brothers and sisters: LaTonya, Margie, Cookie, Jamilia and Mandela. Our father is always looking down on us, and he wants you to know that he loves us all and to be free in who we are. I love you. All of my aunts and uncles both living and deceased.

All of my cousins who were there for me when I had absolutely nothing, especially Kenny McKenzie, Bobby Nelson and Tyrone (Tilt). My friends who were there for me during my early years in the Seattle foster care system: Donovan Hall, Tyler Davis, Curtis Bellinger and Danny Poinier, along with their mothers. Without the love you gave me I can honestly say I would not be here today. Love you guys!

To my Psychology Professor, Mr. Jefferies, my English Professor, Mr. Silverman, and all the staff at Seattle Central Community College. I sincerely thank you for all of your encouragement.

To my Queen, Sebia Green, and daughter, O'Shai Spriggs. Thank you for your unwavering support, understanding and love. We're gonna be alright! I Love You.

To my son, Prince Royale' Armanee Patrick I. You are a hierarchy Leo. You were born to lead. You are the best son any man could ever ask for. You are smarter, stronger and even better looking than me. You have done everything I have ever asked you to do, and I thank you for being such a blessing in my life. Never stop learning, never stop seeking excellence. Be strong, Son, and protect our legacy, for you will be king one day! Your father, King Eric I.

To The Title Holders - (The Don) Ben, (The First Knight) JW, (The Brown Knight) Smoke, (The Count Alexander) Kevin, (The Count) Dante, (The Mobster) Braezy, (The Earl) KK, and all of the Title Holder Women. Aim for the stars, you must be the best, don't settle for less. Be ready always, for we are ranked #1. Much love from your King Eric I.

# ACKNOWLEDGEMENTS

I would like to acknowledge the following people, whose hard work and encouragement has meant so much to me:

My old school partner, Wesley, his wife Carolyn, and Don.

My publisher, Celeste Bennett, and artist, Julie Kim.

Dr. John Cahill and the staff at Children's Orthopaedic Hospital, who in 1972 saved the life of a two-year old boy who had been given lye in his bottle. Thank you for saving me.

Mr. and Mrs. Roebuck, who brought me home with them straight from the hospital.

Sheryl A. Glass, my manager and administrator. Thank you for investing!

To Seattle to Ballard to the Central District to Skyway, I am proud to call you my homeland. Embrace our intelligence, our imaginations, and our dreams and always aim for the stars in whatever we do. Whether it's singing a song, playing sports, or academics give it your all. Do not settle for less!

Without God, I could do nothing.

King Eric I

# CONTENTS

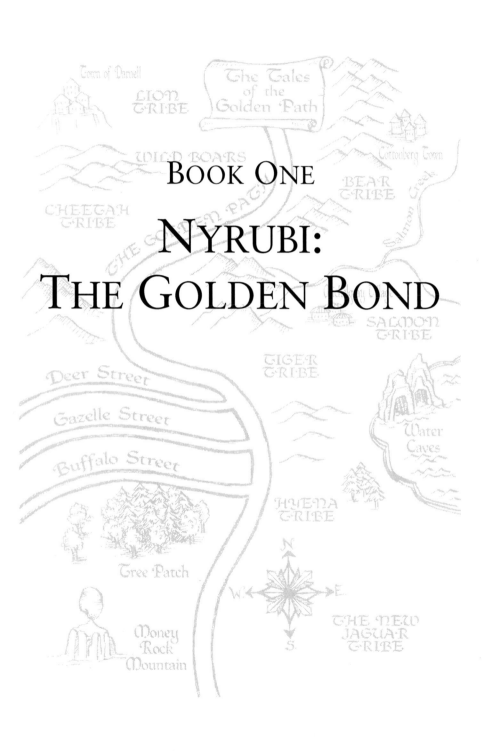

# BOOK ONE

# NYRUBI:
# THE GOLDEN BOND

# PREFACE

**B**ook One of this volume opens seventy years into the history of The Golden Path, when tribes living within its boundaries are established on their new lands and practiced in their laws and regulations. Their collective future, however, is about to be shaken by events from The Golden Path's past.

eventy years ago the land was dark and desolate. Food and water were nearly non-existent, and tribes were at war. Virtually everyone was fighting for their lives. There were no laws, no one was in control and there was no one to stop people from doing anything they wanted to other people, including killing them. That was life in the place called the Planet of the Land of the Seven.

Some tribes were at war with each other for food, some for land, and others for religious domination. These wars had been going on for more than seven years when a man from the Deer Tribe, Comboos, returned from one of his many mysterious spiritual journeys. That trip proved to be the one to finally change life as they knew it.

Comboos was The Peace Keeper. He had been on this particular quest for the last four years. Finally he had come home with great news for everyone. He had discovered a huge land of beauty, richness and abundance where each of the tribes could live upon its own land. In this new land of peace each tribe would not only have their own land, that land would provide them with all of their needs and then some. No more fear of starving to death, no more fighting for scraps, no more freezing in the winter and burning up in the summer from lack of shelter, no more watching their children suffer. There would be plenty of food, and good water. He went on to say, "This place is far from here, but for all that it offers, the long journey is well worth it."

All but one of the tribes was happy about the prospect of a new and peaceful life. The Tiger Tribe was the lone standout. The last thing the Tiger Tribe's ruler, Queen Mayan wanted was peace. You see, for her, war was quite lucrative. She was making big money by training and selling mercenaries for the wars. Queen Mayan surmised that for her and her tribe, the more conflict and war the better. So when Comboos the Peace Keeper spoke of the plans he had for the new land, he emphasized the fact that there would be no more war. Queen Mayan was adamant that the plan would never be realized. The only way to insure business continued "as usual" was for the Peace Keeper to die. Queen Mayan devised and executed a plan to have The Peace Keeper assassinated and make certain that the Jaguar Tribe would be charged for the crime.

# THE TITLE HOLDER GAMES

Before he was assassinated, Comboos set forth rules that would guide the tribes in their new world.

1. No animals are to be killed on The Golden Path.
2. No person is to kill or be killed on The Golden Path.
3. No one is to put in an order to kill unless it is needed to prevent and correct wrongdoing.
4. No tribe is to go to war with another tribe unless they first go in front of the Council, and the Peace Keeper.
5. All Title Holders from all tribes must compete in the title Holder Games once they turn sixteen years of age.

Comboos also established The Title Holder Games, a competition that would help the tribes to establish leadership without war.

People eligible for the Title Holder Games are those who hold or are intended to hold a prominent title (i.e. future King, Queen, Prince, Princess, Earl, Duke, Prime Minister, Lady, etc.) When a Title Holder turns sixteen, they are required to compete in games of strength, endurance, wisdom and courage. All tribes along The Golden Path **must** compete in the games.

The Golden Path's Council and the Peace Keeper are the judges of the Title Holder Games. The Council of The Golden Path consists of the leaders of the Lion, Tiger, Bear and Salmon Tribes. Each tribe speaks their own language, but within seconds of the tribes assembling under the Council they use a universal speech. In addition to judging the Title Holder Games, the Council legislates the rule of the land and has its own army. If a Title Holder refuses to compete in the games, they are banned from their tribe and forever embedded into the Council's Army, remaining in a subordinate position.

The Peace Keeper is the only person who can make it official for a person to become King after they compete in the games.

# DAR-BOO

The Peace Keeper is always drawn from the Deer Tribe. After Comboos' murder, his son became Peace Keeper. At the telling of this story, it is Comboos' great-grandson, Dar-boo, who is the Peace Keeper.

Dar-boo respects his great grandfather's rule of competition. He believes, as did his great grandfather, that all tribes descend from royalty. Comboos created the Title Holder Competition so that the best and royal qualities of each generation would be maintained in the next generation, without resorting to war.

Dar-boo is much more powerful than his great grandfather because he knows more about the different tribal cultures and their leaders. Despite this, he is in the same position as his great-grandfather in that some of the leaders are his friends and some are his enemies, who would love nothing more than to do away with him.

# KING ZHUAN

The Lion Tribe is the largest and strongest tribe on The Golden Path. They provide iron, steel and metals to make weapons, and they trade throughout the tribes. The Lion Tribe is industrialized. They possess the greatest weapons and the most highly skilled army.

King Zhuan has served his people well for over thirty-five years. He is the king of the Lion Tribe, who was crowned when he was only seven years of age. He grew into a great leader. Tall and muscular with a broad chest, his deep voice commands respect.

As the king of his tribe, his life was one of absolute privilege. He had dozens of servants of different ethnicities who tended to his every need and whim, and some of them he genuinely loved. But one thing always disturbed him about his servants: they were not treated well by some of the palace staff. Although it was known that there were loving relationships between some of the royals, staff and servants, they were not allowed to interact publicly or even acknowledge the relationship. Romantic relationships with persons outside of your race were strictly prohibited.

King Zhuan had one child, a daughter named Nyrubi. King Zhuan wanted the best for his daughter: strength, morals, knowledge and wisdom. He set out to give her the best education available.

The best way to do this was to send her to another place, and another time. The Golden Path tribes had vessels that allowed them to travel through time as well as space. King Zhuan arranged for Nyrubi to travel in a time vessel to a school that would prepare her to rule their tribe.

One day King Zhuan of the Lion Tribe went to speak with the Council of The Golden Path. He made the following statement, "In seven days I will take some of my army down to the Hyena Territory and give them a speech." He felt that he should first try diplomacy before war. In this speech he would address the matter of the Hyena Tribe running rampant through The Three Streets, hurting people and taking more than their share of food. "The food supply belongs to all of the tribes and must last until the next shipment. Therefore, the Hyena Tribe must pay the Council of The Golden Path for the stolen food as well as taxes and fines. If they do not do this then I will call for the Council to censure the Hyena Tribe and Chancellor Shenot."

Seven days finally passed, and it came time for King Zhuan to go to the Hyena Tribe and deliver his speech. He knew that the Hyena Tribe did not take kindly to the fact that the Lion Tribe was to be permitted safe entry into their territory, but that did not deter him. He travelled with his army and various Council representatives, covering the distance to the Hyena Tribe in record time.

The Hyena Tribe was already furious over King Zhuan's mere presence, and they become even more steamed as he delivered his speech from the podium. "Your recklessness has jeopardized every tribe among The Golden Path. Your carelessness on The Three Streets has caused chaos. The Council and my tribe, the Lion Tribe, feel that we must put a stop to this behavior. So as of this moment a curfew is now imposed on you, the Hyena Tribe. You will no longer be permitted on The Three Streets—Buffalo Street, Deer Street or Gazelle Street—between the hours of 7:00 p.m. and 7:00 a.m. If caught on these three streets between these hours, you will be found guilty of disobeying the rules of the High Council. The sentence for this offense is death."

Chancellor Shenot looked up at the Lion Tribe's king in utter disbelief and horror. His thoughts were quickly disrupted by his army head, Fanzar. Fanzar angrily said to his leader, "Are we to just sit by and let him tell us what we will and will not do? I say kill him here and now!"

Chancellor Shenot quickly silenced Fanzar. "You fool! If we were to kill him right now in front of the Council and his army the entire Golden Path would come against us, and we would surely be annihilated."

After a moment, Chancellor Shenot continued, "There is another way. For now we will comply with the rules they have imposed against us. We will devise a plan to execute at a later date when they

4

will be caught off guard. This plan will do away with the mighty King Zhuan of the Lion Tribe and his entire family. So be patient my friend. In the meantime prepare yourself and the army and be ready to move on my order."

And then he said to those around him, "My loyal family, join me in a feast while we watch this feeble minded, poor excuse of a leader, King Zhuan, mumble in an attempt to intimidate and control us. It is quite apparent that he is enjoying himself."

Chancellor Shenot muttered under his breath, "Do enjoy this moment of control and power King Zhuan, because this will be your last."

❈

## QUEEN NSTAR

Queen Nstar of the Tiger Tribe was the only person, outside the conspirators, who knew of the plot to kill the Lion Tribe's royal family, though she was only a little girl at the time. She was playing in the woods outside of her palace, when she overheard a conversation between the Wild Boar Tribe's Prince Donshu and the Hyena Tribe's Supreme Ruler, Chancellor Shenot. They were discussing how they would go about the matter of killing King Zhuan and his family.

Shenot told Donshu that if he was successful the Hyena Tribe would grant the Wild Boar Tribe their own land in four years instead of the seven years the Council had said they must wait.

The Council had voted to give the Wild Boar Tribe their own land if they held to certain conditions. Those conditions were distasteful to the Wild Boar Tribe—they demanded no trouble for seven years.

Prince Donshu, the leader of the Wild Boar Tribe, was angry about the way his people were treated. He felt his father, King Grandto, had been tricked by the Council regarding the way they were to receive their own land. Donshu promised himself his people would live on The Golden Path even if they had to take it by force. So Donshu made a deal with the Chancellor of the Hyena Tribe to kill King Zhuan and his royal family.

Queen Nstar only understood what she had heard after the plot to kill King Zhuan had been discovered and one of his family members convicted of conspiracy. Chancellor Shenot and Prince Donshu had avoided prosecution, and when the young Queen Nstar told her family about the conversation she had overheard, either they did not believe her or they felt it was unsafe to allow such a young girl to testify against two powerful tribal leaders.

Queen Nstar also knew that it was her great-grandmother, Queen Mayon, had killed Comboos the first Peace Keeper, but she told no one. In that case, there was too much at stake for her family and her tribe. Queen Nstar felt badly for the Jaguar Tribe, which was falsely convicted of the crime and banned from The Golden Path, and she knew she would tell the truth someday. Queen Nstar promised herself she would one day go outside The Golden Path to find the Jaguar Tribe, bring them back to The Golden Path, and set the record straight.

⊠

## NYRUBI

King Zhuan's daughter Nyrubi was the light of his life. She was happy and fun-loving, yet smart. She loved playing with her cousins— the twins, Sebnala and Teela—and her friend Leo-Paul. Nyrubi made everyone feel like they were somebody and never looked down on anyone, although she was next in line to rule the Lion Tribe.

The plot to assassinate King Zhuan failed, but tragedy did visit his family. When Nyrubi was six, she was on her way to school in the Real World, and her time vessel crashed. It was assumed that she was dead. No one knew that out of eight people onboard the time vessel, there had been one survivor. The one survivor was Nyrubi.

A member of the Jaguar Tribe named Moo-su had found Nyrubi. Moo-su did not know where Nyrubi was from, but she took her in as if Nyrubi was one of her own.

Moo-su was the wife of the Prime Minister of the Jaguar Tribe, Comezar. Comezar had been killed in the tree top war against the Cheetah Tribe, when Moo-su was five months pregnant. When Comezar's son was born, Moo-su named him Afro-Light. Afro-Light was the same age as Nyrubi.

Moo-su raised Afro-Light to follow in his father's footsteps and become Prime Minister of the Jaguar Tribe. Afro-Light is smart and strong, and wants to become nothing less than a great warrior, like his father. Moo-su always told Afro-Light, "Don't worry about what happened in the past. The truth will come to light." But Afro-Light was tired of living in an inhospitable land. He felt his people should be living on the Golden path like the other tribes.

As Afro-Light became a young man he and Nyrubi became the best of friends. They both knew they were from different tribes, but it didn't matter; they still grew close to each other.

Nyrubi was there when Afro-Light graduated, when he went into the military, and when he became Military Sergeant at age sixteen.

# Sebnala and Teela

Sebnala was Nyrubi's cousin and her best friend. She was the daughter of King Zhuan's doctor and King Zhuan's second cousin, Carmleah. Sebnala was very hurt when she was six years of age and heard about the time vessel crash that had taken Nyrubi away.

Sebnala's mother, Carmleah, was second cousin to the King. Since Nyrubi was not present Sebnala was next in line for the crown. Carmleah was the one banned from the Lion Tribe after being found guilty of conspiracy to assassinate King Zhuan and his family.

Teela is the jealous twin sister of Sebnala; jealous because she was not born first. Being firstborn would have made her heir to the throne of the Lion Tribe. Instead, her weak-minded sister Sebnala, who was born first by only seven minutes, would be the next ruler of the Lion Tribe.

Sebnala had to leave the Lion Tribe, because one night someone tried to kill her. Sebnala was saved by her servant, Shar-nu, and a guard named Tryumph. They ran for their lives. They knew they would have to enter another tribe's territory. The cost of being caught trespassing on another tribe's land was either death or a lifetime of slavery.

# Sebnala meets
# Queen Nstar of the Tiger Tribe

When Sebnala, Shar-nu and Tryumph entered the Tiger Tribe's territory, they were captured and taken in front of the Queen. Sebnala was ready to accept her fate, but Queen Nstar knew of Sebnala's importance. She intervened and that evening had Sebnala brought to her chambers. Later that night Queen Nstar started talking to Sebnala, and the conversation lasted through the night.

One of the things Queen Nstar talked to Sebnala about was what she had heard in the woods ten years before. Two men whom she knew were talking and she heard everything they said. She told Sebnala the two men were full of rage, yet as they got deeper into the discussion they became quite happy. These men had plotted to kill King

Zhuan and his family and had discussed rigging the time vessel that would carry Nyrubi to school.

Sebnala screamed with rage. The Queen's people thought Sebnala was going to attack her, so they lunged at Sebnala. The Queen quickly intervened and shouted to the guards to let her be. Sebnala fell to her knees with tears of anger and pain. Sebnala told Queen Nstar she must return to her tribe with the news.

Queen Nstar told Sebnala, "No you must not go back now. They will have you killed. You are welcome to stay here, and you must."

Queen Nstar told Sebnala, "You must go to the Old Land and find out where Nyrubi's time vessel crashed. You must find out whether anyone survived the time vessel crash."

Queen Nstar also told Sebnala she would send three of her best warriors to go and inform King Zhuan. "Don't worry about your people. Go and find the time vessel crash. If you are successful, I will tell you more about the past of The Golden Path and the Old Land. I also will tell you the names of the two men who plotted to kill the king."

## The Search for Nyrubi

As Sebnala, Shar-nu, and the others began the search, Shar-nu realized the next day was Sebnala's birthday. She and Teela, her twin sister, would be sixteen.

Sebnala and the others were the only ones who went on a quest to find Nyrubi. Queen Nstar, had told them it would take at least seven days before they would be in the Old Land, where folktales said the crash had occurred.

The first night Sebnala and the others went through sandstorms. The second night they stopped the big monkeys from killing the little monkeys, and they made a friend, a little monkey named Zet. The third night they all had to work together to get food. The fourth night Zet lead them to the time vessel crash site. The fifth night the search went deeper into the dark and old land. The sixth night the search team was captured by a tribe they had never seen before. On the seventh day, they saw a girl they thought was Nyrubi.

Shar-nu and Sebnala had not seen Nyrubi in ten years, so they couldn't really know if the girl they saw was Nyrubi unless they got a chance to speak to her. They began to approach her, but were immediately captured by guards whom they had not seen.

Their captors led them away. They knew neither where they were going nor what would happen to them. They were led through a water cave, and heard one guard say to the others, "I've heard of this place. This is where all the tribes came through together when they left the Old Land for The Golden Path." The guard stopped and pointed to drawings and marks on the way, "See, this tells the story. The Peace Keeper had given King Zhuan's father the map and the rules of The Golden Path before he was assassinated. The Jaguar Tribe was convicted of the murder. The decision to banish the Jaguar Tribe and leave them behind in the Old Land was made by a vote of all the tribes. All the other tribes except the Elephant Tribe and the Gorilla Tribe, moved to The Golden Path, but the Jaguar Tribe was left behind in the Old Land. The first day after the rest of the tribes had left, the Jaguar Tribe was attacked by the Gorilla Tribe, an attack that lasted for two days and two nights."

## CAPTURED BY THE JAGUAR TRIBE

After the search team was captured and taken to the end of the water cave, they began to see things they had never seen before in their lives. They saw no water, no fields of crops and no sign of many tribes. They were in the Old Land where all the tribes used to live before they moved to The Golden Path.

The leader of the tribe who captured Sebnala and the others told his men to cover the captives' eyes because he did not want them to know where they were going. When Sebnala's eyes were uncovered she and the others were in front of a tribe they had never seen before. The people seemed very angry.

Someone stepped up and spoke, "Who sent you? Why are you here?" The man speaking was Day-shine, the acting Prime Minister of the Jaguar Tribe.

Day-shine is the brother of Comezar and uncle to Afro-Light. Day-shine knows that when Afro-Light is ready for the job of Prime Minister he will have to step down, but Day-shine does not want to give up the post. Day-shine does not want anything to do with The Golden Path. He thinks his people are better off in the Old Land, and he forbids anyone from the Jaguar Tribe to go and see The Golden Path.

As Nyrubi and Moo-su join the rest of the Jaguar Tribe to confront the search team, Day-shine looks at the three guards and says, "Speak!"

Sebnala begins to say, "We are from the ... "

Just as she was going to tell Day-shine the truth, Shar-nu quickly interrupts, saying, "We were looking for food. We did not know we had entered your land. If we have done anything to offend you we are truly sorry."

Day-shine ordered the search team to be taken to the cave. As Sebnala, Shar-nu, and the others are escorted to the dark cave Sebnala speaks in a whispered fury with Shar-nu, "Why did you interrupt me?"

"I did not want them to know where we are from just now."

"Why not?" Sebnala said.

"Because I saw something back there when the other tribe surrounded us. I saw two women, and one of them could be Nyrubi. I think she is Nyrubi."

Sebnala knew only one thing: if Shar-nu was right, she had to get Nyrubi's attention, tell her who they really were and that they had come there to find her and take her back home if she wished.

Sebnala said to Shar-nu, "What if Nyrubi does not remember us?"

"We will first talk to the woman who was standing next to the girl that might be Nyrubi. If Nyrubi trusts her, I think we can. She can help us I think."

The next day the search team received a visitor. It was Afro-Light. The search team came up to the front of the cave jail to have a look at him and hear what he had to say.

Afro-Light told them, "My tribe thinks you all are from another tribe who is our enemy. Furthermore, we believe you are getting ready to attack us. My tribe thinks we should kill you all. I can help you, but I cannot help thinking you are here for another reason. So if there is something you need to tell me, now is the time to do so."

Sebnala told Afro-Light, "If we tell you where we are from you must let us talk to the older woman who was with the younger girl."

Afro-Light charged the cave with rage, "How do you know that girl?"

"I will tell you when we can talk to the older woman," Sebnala said.

"The older woman you wish to speak to is my mother, Moo-su, wife of Comezar the first great Prime Minister of the Jaguar Tribe. My mother has seen and been through a lot. If you bring her harm in any way, I will bring harm to all of you."

Sebnala's guard, Tryumph, walked up to the front of the cave and said to Afro-Light, "I know of your father Comezar. He was as great a leader as he was a warrior. Where we are from my people study his philosophy of war and his study of diversity. It is a great honor to meet you; to be in the presence of Comezar's son."

Afro-Light was in awe as he walked towards Tryumph. He recognized him now as the three-fingered warrior who had been described in great war stories. "Thank you. I have longed to meet you too."

Afro-Light, addressing the search team, spoke again with authority. "If anyone comes to talk to you about where you are from, just tell them you were looking for food and didn't know you were in a tribal territory. That will give me some time with my mother, so we can talk about this matter. I will get back with you in one day. For now, goodbye."

Sebnala looked at Shar-nu, "Do you think we did the right thing?"

"There is no other way. This is right. I recognize something in that girl. If she is Nyrubi and she trusts Afro-Light's mother, I think we can trust her too."

Shar-nu told the search team, "We should feel great! We may have found what we were looking for. If these are our last days, then I am grateful to spend them with you. Thank you for letting me get to know you."

♏

One of the three guards who had accompanied Afro-Light to the cave told Day-shine about what he had heard.

"Tell me everything," Day-shine said to the guard, whose name was Canbe.

"They will not tell us about themselves until they have an opportunity to speak with Moo-su, so we know little about them. Afro-Light, though, spoke about his father with one of the men, who said he knew Comezar."

"How do they know of my brother, Comezar?"

"It is not clear, but I believe that one of them has fought by his side."

Day-shine began pacing. "I will go see Moo-su and tell her I will handle the refugees myself. I will make them talk and tell us where they are from."

⊞

After visiting the prisoners, Afro-Light went in search of his mother, Moo-su. He found her at home, seated with Nyrubi. "Mother," he said, "I must speak with you, alone."

Moo-su looked up from her reading, "Afro-Light is something wrong? Because whatever it is, I am sure Nyrubi can hear it too."

"No, Mother," Afro-Light said, shaking his head. "We must speak alone."

Moo-su nodded, as she excused herself from Nyrubi. "Let us walk into the next room, son."


"Mother," Afro-Light said, "the trespassers wish to speak with you. They tell me that before they can say where they are from— before they will say anything—they have to speak with you."

"Whatever could they want?"

"I do not know, and they refuse to say. They do not seem dangerous, but they are in earnest."

"And do you recommend I see them?"

"I do."

"Very well. I will see them tomorrow morning. However, if this is some kind of game I will have them done away with for good."

⊞

After Afro-Light and Moo-su finished talking, Day-shine entered the room, nodding briefly to both. "Moo-su, I have heard the refugees are making a ridiculous demand. Do not bother yourself with them. On behalf of the tribe, I will see that they talk."

"They wish to speak with me," said Moo-su, "and I intend to speak with them in the morning."

"I am the acting Prime Minister," said Day-shine. "If they wish to say something, then I should be there on behalf of the Jaguar Tribe."

"Day-shine," said Afro-Light, "I will soon be of age to take my father's place as Prime Minister."

"Yes, Afro-Light, you will be Prime Minister. But for now, I will run the tribe as I see fit."

Afro-Light began to approach Day-shine, but he was cut short by Moo-su, who stepped between the two men. With authority in her voice she ended the conversation. "My powers with the Jaguar Tribe are unlimited, for my people love me. I will go see the refugees alone tomorrow."

After Day-shine left the room, Moo-su told Afro-Light to go and get all of his faithful guards. "Pull them aside and tell them to prepare for our defense. I don't trust Day-shine, and if he tries to interfere with the refugees we will need their help."

The next morning Moo-su rose early and walked to the cave. "I am Moo-su, wife of Comezar the great Prime Minister of the Jaguar Tribe. Which one of you wishes to speak with me?"

Sebnala, who had been resting near the entrance, was the first to see Moo-su approaching. "We all wish to speak with you. When we first arrived here we saw you with another girl, whom we believe is of our tribe. We are not refugees. We are a search team looking for a little girl who was lost in a time vessel crash about ten years ago. That little girl should be sixteen now, like Shar-nu, and myself."

Moo-su said, "Where are you from?"

Sebnala glanced at the rest of the search team.

"We are from a place far from here, a place of plenty. We are from the Lion Tribe, and our land is on The Golden Path."

Moo-su excited, stepped forward, "The Golden Path! In our tribe, we have not spoken of The Golden Path in seventy years. You mustn't tell anyone else where you are from. For now, tell me more about the little girl."

"The little girl was King's Zhuan's daughter, Nyrubi. We want to find her and let her know we love her. We hope she will go home, to The Golden Path."

Shar-nu added, "Lady Moo-su, we wanted to speak with you because if the girl we saw with you is Nyrubi, and we have reason to believe she is, then it is apparent Nyrubi trusts you. We feel we can trust you too. We didn't know how to go about making sure that was Nyrubi without alarming anyone else."

Sebnala asked Moo-su, "Is the girl Nyrubi, or will you not tell us?"

Moo-su said, "First I will speak with my son, Afro-Light, and let him make the decision about the girl whom you call Nyrubi."

Moo-su walked away feeling happy to know someone could tell Nyrubi about her true home. Moo-su said to herself, "This could be something great."

Moo-su returned home and found Afro-Light and Nyrubi enjoying dinner together. "Afro-Light, I would like to talk with you alone."

Nodding, Afro-Light followed his mother to a room nearby, where she told him of her meeting.

"I have something to talk to you about the people who we are holding. They say they are here to find a girl … "

"What girl?" Afro-Light said.

"The girl they call Nyrubi. Nyrubi is from a place we don't talk about around here. Nyrubi is from The Golden Path."

"What and where is The Golden Path?"

"I will tell you later, but for now we must see if the girl they are speaking about is really Nyrubi. If she is then we must let her see them. Nyrubi is the great King Zhuan's daughter and the future Queen of the Lion Tribe. The people we are holding want to speak with her.

"Afro-Light I would like to leave it up to you to decide. You must tell Nyrubi that some people would like to talk to her."

Afro-Light asked his mother, "How will I know what is the right thing to do?"

"You will make the right decision. I trust you, Afro-Light."

Afro-Light returned to the room where Nyrubi remained, waiting for his return. Seeing him, Nyrubi immediately knew something was wrong. "What is the matter? Tell me, Afro-Light, so I can help you."

Afro-Light, kneeling to hold Nyrubi's hands, began. "The people who we are holding say they are looking for a girl who was lost in a time vessel crash ten years ago … The little girl they are looking for is you, Nyrubi. Yes, you."

Nyrubi said out loud, "Why me?"

Afro-Light said, "My mother had told me she found you, but she never told me where she found you. There are a lot of things you and I don't know, but I think it would be a good thing for you to know where you are from and who you really are. Tomorrow I will go with you to see and speak with the search team."

Nyrubi was visibly upset. "What if I don't want to speak with them? What if I am happy here? I don't care about where I am from."

"Nyrubi," Afro-Light said gently, "think about it tonight, and try to think about it with an open mind. These people have risked their lives to find you. I can only wish that if something happened to me someone would love me enough to fine me. Give them a chance to talk to you."

The night was long for the search team. Sebnala and the others were awaiting the morning light to herald the day they might speak with the girl whom they had been seeking; their childhood friend, whom they had not seen in ten years.

It was 7:00 in the morning when Nyrubi and Afro-Light arrived at the cave. All was quiet. Sleep had overtaken all but one of the anxious search team. Only the servant Shar-nu was awake.

Upon seeing her, Shar-nu knew she was seeing Nyrubi. Moreover, Nyrubi felt somehow that she knew Shar-nu.

The quiet greetings of Shar-nu and Nyrubi awoke the others.

Sebnala greeted Nyrubi next. "How are you, Nyrubi? You are so pretty."

Nyrubi felt her defenses rise. "How do you know my name is Nyrubi?"

"How do you know if Nyrubi is your real name?"

"I just do. Do not ask me any questions. I ask you the questions." This silenced Sebnala.

Nyrubi look at Afro-Light and then said to Sebnala, "Why are you looking for me? Tell me now!"

Sebnala told Nyrubi, "Do you know of a man named King Zhuan?"

"This King Zhuan, is he a great man or something?" Nyrubi asked.

"Yes, he is." Sebnala began telling Nyrubi, "King Zhuan is the king of the powerful Lion Tribe, which is on The Golden Path." And Sebnala described The Golden Path to Nyrubi. "King Zhuan is your father. He misses you very much."

"My father ... " Nyrubi replied, as she searched her earliest memories.

Sebnala told Nyrubi, "Right now, as we speak, there is a plot to assassinate him and usurp his throne. He knows of this. Nyrubi, you are next in line to rule the powerful Lion Tribe. There are people who believe you are alive and have sent us to find you. We have come to ask you to return with us and claim your rightful place. It is urgent. You must return to your homeland and compete in the Title Holder Games. We can take you there, but we must leave at once. if you don't want to come back can you make sure we can be let free to return to our home?"

Nyrubi told Sebnala "I can't make that decision."

Afro-Light said, "I will give you my word. Nyrubi and I will see you again after we talk to my mother, Moo-su."

▦

As Afro-Light, and Nyrubi walked away Afro-Light asked Nyrubi whether she understood what and who the captives had been speaking about. "This King Zhuan, who they say is your father, do you remember him?"

"Afro-Light, I need some time to think about all of this."

"I understand."

Nyrubi awoke when it was dark and the night frogs could be heard. She remembered her father. Silently, she rose and made her way to Moo-su's room.

"Moo-su, Moo-su," Nyrubi wept, "I remember my father. You must tell me about my childhood."

Moo-su told Nyrubi how she had found her among the wreckage of a time vessel. "You remembered only your name," said Moo-su, as she smoothed Nyrubi's hair. "These are the first people to have spoken of the crash. Perhaps the vessel did come from the Lion Tribe."

Nyrubi was silent.

Moo-su said, "Do you want to find your real people and learn where you are from? I think I would like to know if it were me. Go tell the two girls, Sebnala and Shar-nu, that you would like to learn more from them if you can."

"Moo-su," asked Nyrubi, "Why aren't you and your tribe living on The Golden Path?"

"That is a long story, and I will tell it to you later. For now, go and tell them you will go with them when they are let free to return to their homeland."

Nyrubi shook her head, "I don't know what I will do when they are set free, but I will go now and listen to the people who came to find me."

"I am glad, child" said Moo-su. "I have an idea. Visit them this morning, and then I will have Afro-Light and his guards bring the two girls here, to join us for dinner tonight. We can have a conversation and get to know each other."

"Thank you, Moo-su," Nyrubi hugged her guardian.

⚏

Nyrubi soon was back at the cave, where she told Sebnala and the others that they will be joining her at Moo-su's home for dinner. "Maybe there we will talk about life, your homeland, and my father."

Shar-nu said to Nyrubi, "Truly I am honored; however, I am part of a team. I cannot eat a meal from the royal table if the rest of my search team does not eat the same."

Nyrubi looked Shar-nu in the eye and said to her, "I am quite impressed with your allegiance and leadership." She then assured them both that not only will the others receive proper food and water, they would be served the same food.

That night at dinner Sebnala, Shar-nu, and Nyrubi talked about the times when they were little, how each other grew up, and how long it took the search team to find Nyrubi.

Moo-su told them about Comezar and, knowing she was speaking with future leaders, she decided to tell the young people about the murder of the Peace Keeper and how the Jaguar Tribe was framed for it. Nyrubi announced to Moo-su and the others at the dinner table that she would someday set the record straight about who did what.

That's when Shar-nu said, "I have an idea. Upon our return to our homeland we are all required to compete in the competition games. I think when we bring Nyrubi back with us she should go in front of the Council and tell them she will not compete with the tribe she is originally from, however, she will compete with the Jaguar Tribe, and that is the only way she will compete in the Title Holder Games."

Nyrubi looked at Moo-su and the others and then said to Shar-nu, "That is a great idea!"

Moo-su said to them all, "Yes it is high time we, the Jaguar Tribe were exonerated for a crime we never committed and released from a penalty we should never have paid. The truth needs to go forth, and my people should be allowed to live like kings and Queens. Furthermore, Comezar would want you, Afro-Light, when you are ready, to go before the Council and defend your tribe. So you go with Nyrubi, Afro-Light, and I will stay here with the Jaguar Tribe until you come back to take us to our rightful home on The Golden Path."

As Nyrubi, Sebnala, and Shar-nu were talking with Moo-su and Afro-Light, who should enter the room but Day-shine.

Day-Shine asked Moo-su, "Why was I not invited to this little dinner?" He abruptly took a seat and sat down at the table.

Moo-su offhandedly addressed Day-shine saying, "Do join us Day-Shine. I thought surely Canbe informed you." She continued to tell the rest at the table what had happened to the Peace Keeper and who might have killed him.

Afro-Light was especially interested in this conversation. All of his life, Afro-Light had heard about the Great Peace Keeper, Comboos, but he had never heard the full story.

Moo-su told them the whole story. Comezar, and Moo-su had known someone set them up for failure. "We were banned from living on The Golden Path for life. My tribe has lived in this dark and desolate Old Land for seventy years. We had to learn how to survive out here. The first ten years my people were put to the test and during those years we lost many of our people."

"Comezar always believed that justice would prevail of its own accord. The evidence against our tribe was circumstantial. Although he knew our people would pay a heavy price, Comezar chose to abide by the Council's judgment. His option would have been to go to war against the Tiger Tribe, to force them into confession. But, he felt, that would only play into our enemy's plan: they had assassinated Comboos to provoke a war. Comezar would always say to me, 'One day the truth will become known.' As Comezar's wife I have always honored his wishes."

The young people gathered around her dinner table were moved by what they heard. Moo-su continued, "Never in my lifetime have I thought I would see The Golden Path, where every tribe has their own land, food, and freedom to worship as they wish. I might never see The Golden Path, but I would like for you, Afro-Light, to see it. And, Nyrubi, that is your homeland. You need to go and see your father. He has missed you for over ten years, and he would be very happy to see you."

Day -Shine said, "I forbid you, Moo-su, to go see The Golden Path."

Moo-su told Day-Shine, "You may tell me that, but not Afro-Light. He may go as he wishes. He is coming of age, and must, as you know compete in the Title Holder Games. You have held the post for him while he is a child, but he will be the new Prime Minister of the Jaguar Tribe."

Day-shine was speechless, and Moo-su immediately turned to Afro-Light, "Take some of our warriors and go with Nyrubi. Afro-Light you must compete. Furthermore you must show all the others who we are, because the rest of the tribes have neither seen nor spoken of us in seventy years. You will be the first Jaguar person they see, so be proud of who you are and of your heritage.

"Go in front of the Council of The Golden Path, and tell them what you know about the killing of Comboos. It may be that nothing will come of this, but you must always remember that your people have endured great hardship because of their faith in justice. Always be proud of yourself and your people, and return to us."

The light of pride shone in Afro-Light's eyes, as he replied. "Mother, I know in my heart that I will honorably set our people free from the Old Land. Our people will resume their rightful place and take up residence on The Golden Path. I am certain that the spirit of my father will help me to lead our people back to their rightful place. Everyone will know the Jaguar Tribe would never kill for no reason. Surely, the killers of the Peace Keeper, Comboos from Deer Street, will be brought to justice, and our tribe exonerated."

It took Nyrubi, Afro-Light and the others eight days to go from the Old Land to The Golden Path.

When they arrived at the palace, Sebnala put Nyrubi in a different room so that King Zhuan could not see her right away.

Sebnala and Shar-nu led the king to the room that Nyrubi was in. The doors opened and for the first time in ten years, the King saw his daughter Nyrubi. The King fell to his knees and cried out to Nyrubi as she ran to his arms.

They stayed in that room for seven hours just talking and talking. Nyrubi told her father she had a friend. "This friend's mother found me after the time vessel crash."

King Zhuan said to Nyrubi, "I am quite anxious to meet this 'friend,' who helped my daughter all of these years, I owe this friend a huge debt of gratitude. But first Nyrubi, there is someone who desperately wants to see you."

Just then a big, strong man walked into the room. King Zhuan said to Nyrubi, "This was your dear friend when you were both little. Do you remember Leo-Paul?"

Nyrubi and Leo-Paul looked at each other with great happiness and joy.

Leo-Paul had been found by King Zhuan many years before on a day the king was swimming in the river. King Zhuan saw something unusual on a log in the water: it was a little boy. "This little boy must have come downstream from the floods," he thought. King Zhuan took the little boy in, treated him like his own, and named him Leo-Paul.

Leo-Paul had been raised with Nyrubi and Sebnala. They had all played together as children, before Nyrubi's time vessel crash. Some had thought Nyrubi and Leo-Paul would be married. After the time vessel crash, Sebnala and Leo-Paul's friendship had grown. Leo-Paul had always wanted Sebnala to come back: he never understood why she left.

By the time he was sixteen, Leo-Paul was bigger than any other member of the Lion Tribe. Even at that age, he had grown into a mature and wise young man. Before he was twenty, he was named General of the Lion Tribe's powerful army. Leo-Paul answered to no one but King Zhuan himself.

Nyrubi told her father and Leo-Paul about the time vessel crash and the person who had found and raised her as if she had been her own child. She told them her name was Moo-su, but Nyrubi did not want them to know Moo-su was from the Jaguar Tribe until Afro-Light was in the room; for she did not know how her father and Leo-Paul would react when they saw a member of the Jaguar Tribe for the first time in seventy years.

"This woman who raised me as her own treated me like a queen even though she had a son who needed her very much. She loved me and helped me become who I am today. Moreover, they have now taught me about this land we call The Golden Path, the good and the bad."

Nyrubi looked at her father, and said, "Please Father do not get angry. Please wait to form your opinion until after you have heard all that needs to be said in this room. What you and Leo-Paul are about to see and hear is going to be very difficult for you."

King Zhuan and Leo Paul looked at each other.

Nyrubi said to her father, "I would like you to meet my friend, Afro-Light. And you too, Leo-Paul, I would like you to meet Afro-Light as well." Nyrubi walked out of the room and into the hallway. Sebnala and Shar-nu were waiting. She asked them to bring Afro-Light into the room.

A few minutes later, Nyrubi, Sebnala, Shar-nu and then Afro-Light entered the room. Leo-Paul was happy to see Sebnala, but his attention was quickly diverted by Afro-Light's entrance. King Zhuan looked at Afro-Light and said loudly, "Where is this person from?"

Nyrubi was just about to tell him when Afro-Light spoke up for himself. "I am from the Jaguar Tribe. I am son of the Comezar, Prime Minister of my people. I am Afro-Light."

Leo-Paul walked up to Afro-Light. The two men squared off face-to-face, as if they were born to fight each other to the death. Leo-Paul said, "I am sure you know that if you or any of your tribe step foot inside The Golden Path you will be killed. I am ready to do so right now."

Afro-Light grasped the dagger at his side. Leo-Paul and Afro-Light were both prepared to fight.

"Stop!" King Zhuan ordered. To Leo-Paul he said, "These people have restored my daughter to our tribe. I want to hear why they have come here." Leo-Paul bowed his head in assent. Without ever turning from Afro-Light, he stepped back to stand beside King Zhuan.

Nyrubi and Sebnala asked King Zhuan to listen carefully to Afro-Light. "He will tell you all that you need to know."

Afro-Light began by telling the king that his people did not have anything to do with the death of Comboos the Peace Keeper. He shared the information his mother had provided and told of the suffering of his people. "My people should not be living in the Old Land, punished for a crime they did not commit. It is our right to live on this Path with the other tribes."

Leo-Paul asked Afro-Light, "Why didn't anyone from your tribe do or say anything seventy years ago?"

"My great-grandfather did not want to live where people were not being true. He believed that, one day, someone would come forward and tell the truth."

Afro-Light continued, "I would like to compete in the Title Holder Games, for I will become the next Prime Minister of the Jaguar Tribe and then set my people free from the Old Land."

King Zhuan had been listening carefully to all Afro-Light said. He thought to himself, *This man is young and eager, but he is honest and brave. What he said holds merit.* When Afro-Light finished speaking King Zhuan said, "I must go in front of the Council and tell them what you have told me."

Leo-Paul was not convinced. He said to Afro-Light, "I do not believe what you say is true, and if the Council determines it is not I will be the one to kill you."

Afro-Light looked at Leo-Paul and said to him, "Or I will kill you."

Leo Paul continued, "But if the Council determines that what you say is true, then I will be among all the people of the Lion Tribe who will welcome you and your tribe back to The Golden Path. Only the Council has the power to determine the truth of your tale."

⊞

King Zhuan sent messengers to convey the news and request a special meeting of the Councilors. All who were able gathered that afternoon.

Nyrubi, Afro-Light and Leo-Paul were welcomed as guests, and then the presiding member opened by saying, "We all know why we are here, thanks to King Zhuan's briefing. As you know, Council law requires full tribal representation on something of such great import. Today, we will not be able to vote because two of our members are missing, but we will accept testimonial and open this matter for discussion and debate."

Another member stated, "One of the missing members is Darboo, the great-grandson of Comboos, whom the Jaguar Tribe killed. I object to this meeting: it is imperative he be present."

Another member said, "For the record, I do not believe it is right for Dar-boo to even see Afro-Light. He has never seen a member of the Jaguar Tribe, in all his life. To bring him face-to-face with a leader of the tribe who murdered his grandfather is unfair."

When their comments were noted in the record, the presiding member allowed Nyrubi's friends to exercise their right to speak on behalf of Afro-Light. Shar-nu and Sebnala told how Afro-Light an his mother had intervened on their behalf when they were prisoners. Even Leo-Paul told the Council that Afro-Light had been a great friend to The Golden Path and to the Lion Tribe. "He saved the searchers who went out looking for Nyrubi. When the Jaguar Tribe wanted to do away with the search team, Afro-Light put his life on the line and set them free." Leo Paul then looked straight at Afro-Light, "And for that, the Lion Tribe, King Zhuan, and myself, are truly, truly, grateful. We are grateful to the Jaguar Tribe, to your mother, and to you, Afro-Light."

King Zhuan then rose to speak. "Fellow Councilors, you know my joy at having my daughter returned. We all share in the happiness of her return. Thank you for gathering to meet her and hear what she has learned during her time with the Jaguar Tribe." He nodded to the presiding Councilor, who then asked Nyrubi to speak to the Council.

Nyrubi rose, and spoke with a strong voice, "I have lived with the Jaguar Tribe for ten years under the guardianship of Moo-Su, wife to the Prime Minister. Never have I heard talk that would implicate them in the death of Comboos. I have come to know and understand their pride and ethics; how they believe that truth and justice will prevail in time. This is why they have not fought in their own defense. I also have seen their suffering in the Old Land, where there is no good food or water. They did not have anything to do with the killing of the Peace Keeper, Comboos. They were set up, and I believe that an open trial will reveal that to be the truth. We have lived bountifully, and they did nothing to deserve such hardship. Surely The Golden Path can afford such mercy and graciousness as to allow them an open hearing."

The Council asked Nyrubi to leave the room so they could discuss the matter in private. They thought Nyrubi spoke well, but there remained the obvious question. If the Jaguar Tribe had not murdered Comboos, then who did? They knew this question would have to be handled with care.

Nyrubi and Afro-Light waited in the antechamber. There was a huge risk to this meeting. If the Council said no to the request and Afro-Light's tribe was still banished, the Council had the right to kill Afro-Light or order him to be put into the Council's Army for life, and he would never see his mother or his tribe again.

⊞

As the Council members were discussing what they had heard, the door to the Council's chamber opened to admit one of the members who had been absent when the meeting convened. She approached the table and remained standing, a signal to the other members that she would like to speak. The Council grew quiet and the newly arrived member spoke, "I know who killed the Peace Keeper. It was not Afro-Light's people. It was mine." This member was the powerful Queen Nstar of the Tiger Tribe.

Queen Nstar told the Council, "My great-grandmother, Queen Mayon, killed Comboos. Queen Mayon was making lots of money making weapons for the war, and then selling them to other tribes. Comboos came up with a peace plan. Queen Mayon did not want peace, so she devised her own plan to kill Comboos. Killing Comboos would insure continuous war and so she would continue to make lots of money."

"We the Council have wronged The Jaguar Tribe, and for that, they should be welcomed to The Golden Path. They also should be able to take my tribe's place on The Golden Path. Moreover, we will go back and live in the Old Land, as they were forced to do for seventy years. This is the right way."

⊞

When Afro-Light was told what Queen Nstar had said, he announced, "I did not come here for revenge or to take another's place. Furthermore, I do not blame you, Queen Nstar, for what your great-grandmother did. What I want is for my tribe to be reinstated with full rights, which includes our right to compete in the Title Holder Games this year."

As Afro-Light was speaking, another man arrived at the Council. It was Dar-boo. He said "I have been listening to what you have said." He then walked up to Nyrubi, Shar-nu, Sebnala and Leo-Paul and said, "The person you have brought in front of the Council is banned from The Golden Path and yet you still believe what he has to say. Your friend should be thankful for that, but I am going to ask you all, do you think the Jaguar Tribe killed my great-grandfather?"

They all said, "No."

Queen Nstar walked up to Dar-boo and said to him, "They did not kill Comboos, Dar-boo. It was my great-grandmother who did, and I, Queen Nstar, am very sorry. I am sorry Dar-boo, and I apologize to you."

Queen Nstar looked at the Council and said, "My tribe is ready for whatever the Council has for us."

Dar-boo told the Council, "There have been enough lies on The Golden Path, and that's why we left the Old Land. Let's put all of this behind us and go on. I do not want the Tiger Tribe to go anywhere. And for the Jaguar Tribe, if they do well in the Title Holder Games then they will be welcomed to The Golden Path. Furthermore, I have the power to say so. Therefore, let it be done."

Queen Nstar looked at Afro-Light and said, "I would like nothing better than to meet your mother, Moo-su, as soon as possible. I regard her as one of the greatest women living today. Go, and bring her to the Council immediately so that we may apologize to her and thank her."

## THE TITLE HOLDER GAMES

The three events in the Title Holder Games were called Tree Wars, River Wild, and Condor Competition. Dar-boo described the events to the participants.

"In The Tree Wars event you all will climb The Royal Tree and perch on branches. Upon the signal given, your goal will be to throw the others from the tree. The only thing that can be used is your body. Hitting and kicking are not allowed. The tree vines can be used to swing from one branch to another. The last five people to remain in the tree move on to the next competition, which is The River Wild."

The competitors remained silent, and Dar-boo continued.

"The River Wild competition is set in the middle of a rushing river. You must get to the other side using only what is available in the vicinity—logs, vines, etc. The river is full of crocodiles and other lethal predators. You cannot go around the river; you must go through it. Your goal is to cross in less than fifteen minutes. No interference with another competitor is allowed. Your competition here are the predators, the current, and the clock."

He paused. "For those of you who continue there will be the Condor Competition. This last and final competition is the most dangerous. It involves bringing back a baby condor. The adult condor has a body length of 43 to 52 inches, a wingspan up to 9.5 feet, and weighs 18-23 pounds. They are deadly and do not take kindly to anyone messing with their babies.

"Your first task will be to locate a nest. Condors prefer mountains. They nest in gorges or caves or clefts among boulders on a cliff or hillside, which create updrafts, thus providing favorable soaring conditions. They can see you coming a mile away, but you cannot see always them.

"The egg is incubated for 54-58 days. The young condor learns to fly in about six months but will stay with its parents for several more months. You are to bring back a condor who has learned to fly but has not yet left the nest. I wish you well."

The competitors prepared themselves, and the games began ...

♜

Afro-Light did well in the Title Holder Games. The top two contenders were Leo-Paul and Afro-Light. This was exactly what everyone had wanted to see:. Who was the strongest between the two? But to everyone's surprise their scores were exactly the same. Sebnala, Teela and Shar-nu, yes Shar-nu, did well in the Title Holder's Games too.

The Peace Keeper Dar-boo revealed to everyone a long held secret about Shar-nu. He said, "My father was the one who helped Shar-nu's mother when she gave birth to a baby girl and would not reveal the name of the father. We all know that your mother was King Zhuan's servant, but not until you were born did your mother tell only my father and me the name of your father.

"I was just a young man and did not fully understand the ramifications of such a secret. Nevertheless I kept the secret all of these years. Under these circumstances it is befitting that I finally reveal the secret for I have come to the conclusion that it will now only bring joy. Shar-nu, the name of your father is none other than the great King Zhuan of the Lion Tribe. Yes, King Zhuan's first child was by his servant, so you and Nyrubi are really half sisters. Moreover, Shar-nu will no longer be addressed as a servant for she has royal blood running through her veins." Dar-boo held her hand and said, "Because of this news she must also compete in the Title Holder Games. The Council has voted on letting the Jaguar Tribe compete in the Title Holder Games. The Council also voted on letting the Tiger Tribe stay too."

After the Title Holder Games, Dar-boo told Afro-Light, "We, the Council, want to give you, your tribe and your mother Moo-su a State Tribe Parade." Dar-boo told Afro-Light, Sebnala, Shar-nu, Nyrubi and Leo-Paul how proud he was of all of them. "I know you will be great leaders."

░

Everything was great on The Golden Path. There was even more to be happy about. Nyrubi married Afro-Light, Sebnala married Leo-Paul, and Shar-nu married Tryumph.

Nyrubi passed up her right to be queen of the Lion Tribe so that she could live with Afro-Light and the Jaguar Tribe. Sebnala became the next in line to the Lion Tribe throne. Shar-nu focused her work on helping children.

And for a long while, they lived happily.

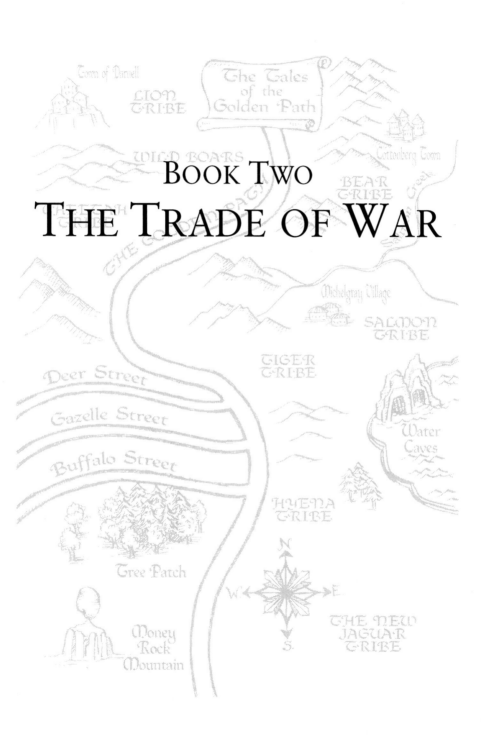

# BOOK TWO
# THE TRADE OF WAR

# PREFACE

When the lands of The Golden Path became known to them, the Cheetah, Lion, Hyena, Bear, Salmon, Tiger and Deer tribes made the decision to make The Golden Path their new home. There were two tribes, however, who voted to remain in the Old Land and forever at war with the tribes of The Golden Path. These were the Elephant Tribe and the Gorilla Tribe.

arly one morning Prince Amtar of the mighty Cheetah Tribe, who was enjoying breakfast with his lovely wife, Graceshell, and his beautiful daughter, Speed-Shay, was surprised to hear his servant report, "There is a visitor who wishes to speak with the prince."

"Who is it?" Prince Amtar asked his servant.

"It is the Peace Keeper, Dar-boo."

Prince Amtar said "Welcome him in. Go, go, and welcome him.

Lady Graceshell turned to their daughter, "Come, let us give the men some time alone."

Prince Amtar told Graceshell, "It is all right, my love. We haven't seen the Peace Keeper in a long time. I am certain Dar-boo would love to see both you and Speed-Shay."

As the Peace Keeper walked into the living quarters, Prince Amtar said, "Welcome Dar-boo! Come and feast with us. The food is still hot, come."

Dar-boo walked up to the prince, and the two men gave each other a hearty hug and Dar-boo asked, "How are you, Lady Graceshell and young Speed-Shay?"

Speed-Shay blushed. "We are doing very well, sir. Thank you for asking."

Lady Graceshell asked, "How are you?" And she gestured for him to join them at the table.

When all of them were seated, Dar-boo began by telling Lady Graceshell, "I'm truly excited about the next Title Holder Games. Only two years, and they will come around again."

Speed-Shay asked her mother if she could ask the Peace Keeper a question.

Graceshell said, "But of course, you can."

Speed-Shay asked "Dar-boo who won the previous Title Holder Game? How did all of the tribes who participated in the games do?"

Dar-boo told the fourteen-year-old Speed-Shay that the last Title Holder Games were special. "Like no other we have ever seen in the seventy-two years that The Golden Path or the games have existed."

"Why is that?" Speed-Shay asked.

Dar-boo said, "Because in the last Title Holder Games we had a participant from the Jaguar Tribe. Their tribe, as you may know, had never been seen on The Golden Path and never been allowed to play in the Title Holder Games. You may not know why that was: it was because they had been convicted—falsely, it turns out—of the assassination of the Great Peace Keeper Comboos, who was my great-grandfather."

Speed-Shay nodded her head in sympathy for the loss of Dar-boo's ancestor, and Dar-boo continued, "Comboos was the person who discovered The Golden Path. That was some seventy-two years ago, before we voted to move to The Golden Path." Dar-boo also told Speed-Shay about Afro-Light, and explained that he is a member of the Jaguar Tribe. "Afro-Light went head-to-head against Leo-Paul, a member of the Lion Tribe, in nearly every event; but Leo-Paul was just a little too much for Afro-Light to handle." The stories continued, and Dar-boo told Speed-Shay about the women of the tribes who had participated in the Title Holder Games. "They also did very well, but once again the women of the Lion Tribe seemed to be too much for the rest of the tribe to keep up with."

"Why was that?" Lady Graceshell asked Dar-boo.

"Well, because the Lion Tribe had a new member enter the games. She was Shar-nu, who was a servant."

Speed-Shay immediately asked, "I thought the Title Holder Games were only for Title Holders, people who held royal positions in a tribe?"

"Shush," Lady Graceshell admonished her daughter. "That will be quite enough."

Dar-boo said to Lady Graceshell, "It is OK. She should know the whole truth if she so desires." Dar-boo said to Speed-Shay, "Well that is true. You must be of royalty to compete in the games. That is why the story of Shar-nu is even more interesting. You see, before the arranged marriage between King Zhuan and Queen Sherlay of the Lion Tribe took place King Zhuan's servant named Geela became pregnant and would not reveal the name of the father. Unaware that Geela was pregnant, King Zhuan left for the warrior quest. When the baby was born Geela revealed to my father and me that the father of the child was King Zhuan. She swore us to secrecy because she did not want to damage the status of the father and bring more scrutiny to her and her child, and then she disappeared, leaving the child with Dar-boo. It was later revealed by myself that the child she was pregnant with was fathered by King Zhuan of the Lion Tribe. So that actually made Shar-nu the eldest child of the royal family, and with royal blood in her veins she was required to compete in the Title Holder Games. Since Shar-nu was conceived outside of marriage she will be in line for the throne behind the legitimate children, so Nyrubi would be first and then Shar-nu."

Dar-boo did not say so, but he had always believed that Shar-nu would play a pivotal role in the continuance of The Golden Path.

Upon Graceshell's asking about Nyrubi, Dar-boo told the story of how Nyrubi was thought to be dead in a time vessel crash she had actually survived; how she was found by the Jaguar Tribe and raised up as one of their own; and how Shar-nu played a role as a member of the Search Team that had found her half-sister, Nyrubi. "Until they found her, she had no memory of being born Princess Nyrubi the daughter of King Zhuan of the Lion Tribe," he explained. Then Dar-boo told Speed-Shay how Shar-nu, Sebnala and her twin sister Teela had dominated the Title Holder Games. "Their individual events as well as their team events were outstanding and no other tribe could match them!"

"Thank you, Dar-boo!" said Speed-Shay, her eyes sparkling.

"You are very welcome," he said. "Someday, you will participate as well."

Speed-Shay beamed.

"And now," said Prince Amtar, "let us retire to my study."

Graceshell excused herself and Speed-Shay as Prince Amtar and Dar-boo walked into the next room where they could talk alone. Dar-boo said to Amtar, "You wanted to speak with me about a matter?"

Prince Amtar replied, "Yes."

"You have my undivided attention," said Dar-boo.

Prince Amtar began telling Dar-boo about when he and his warriors were on their annual Warrior Quest. "One of my men noticed something in the sky."

"In the sky?" Dar-boo said.

"Yes, I am sure of it," Amtar said to Dar-boo. "It looked like some kind of huge monkey with wings. It had something, or someone riding on the back of it. There were seven of them flying above us. I have never seen anything like this before, so I felt I should tell someone about what I saw."

Dar-boo looked at Prince Amtar and said, "That is very strange, because ever since we all moved to The Golden Path we have only been at war with the Elephant Tribe, and the Gorilla Tribe, and we always had victory. The Lion Tribe, Tiger Tribe, and Bear Tribe told me the last time they were attacked by the Elephant and Gorilla Tribes they had someone new on their side. Someone or something so new, that our tribes from The Golden Path could not defend themselves and had to retreat.

Prince Amtar then asked Dar-boo, "How is King Zhuan of the Lion Tribe?"

Dar-boo said, "It has been awhile since I have seen King Zhuan, but he was doing fine the last time we met."

Prince Amtar said to Dar-boo, "Please tell everyone hello for me."

Dar-boo responded, "You may get the chance to tell them yourself if the Council asks for all the tribes to meet at once, but for now Prince Amtar I shall be leaving. I'll speak with you again soon."

Prince Amtar said, "If there is anything I or my tribe can do just say the word and I will be there."

Somewhere in the old land were the Elephant, and Gorilla Tribes territory is located, there was another meeting taking place. This meeting was attended by only the Elephant Tribe, the Gorilla Tribe and the Invaders.

The Invaders are the figures Prince Amtar was describing to Dar-boo on that same morning. They are ten feet tall and talk with a voice like the wind. They cannot be killed by any man. There are only seven, but they are powerful and ride on the backs of winged baboons capable of terrorizing the tribes of The Golden Path. They call themselves The Game Hunters.

The Game Hunters are from a foreign land, and their goal is to take The Golden Path away from the tribes that live there. Moreover the Invaders plan to do away with the men and sell them as slaves. The Game Hunters would like nothing more than to get rid of the men of The Golden Path so they could have the women of The Golden Path to themselves. They believe this is the only way their race will survive, and if they can mate with the women of The Golden Path, their offspring would become the next generation of The Golden Path.

They called the meeting with the Elephant and Gorilla Tribes to present a plan whereby they would start trouble with each tribe while making it look like another tribe was responsible for the deed. If they were successful, the tribes of The Golden Path would soon be at war with each other, making it that much easier for them to be conquered.

The Game Hunters knew they needed the Elephant and the Gorilla Tribe as their army, to carry out all of the dirty work to be done against the tribes of The Golden Path. The Elephant and Gorilla Tribes wanted the tribes of The Golden Path to serve them, and they knew they needed the Game Hunters for their strategy and leadership if they were to accomplish their goal. The Invader made a deal with both of the tribes to take over The Golden Path. Upon coming to an agreement, the Game Hunters began to describe their plan, which would start with tricking the Bear Tribe ...

It is up to the Peace Keeper and the tribes of The Golden Path to figure out exactly how they can kill an Invader, if it is even possible to kill an Invader.

⬤

As Peace Keeper, Dar-boo went to see the Council as soon as he arrived home. Dar-boo told the Council that there had been sightings of some unfamiliar men on The Golden Path. "We expect they were the one who helped the Gorilla and the Elephant tribe successfully win the battle of Hill Canon against the Lion, Bear and Tiger tribes. We must be safe. Call a meeting of all the tribes of The Golden Path to warn them of a possible attack and encourage unity among our tribes. It is going to take all of the tribes working together to defeat these unknown invaders."

One member of the Council said to Dar-boo, "How do we know if these so called Invaders have not come here to help us?"

Dar-boo replied, "Prince Amtar of the Cheetah Tribe has seen the Invader flying over him and his army, and from the way he describes them it did not seem like they were trying to be anybody's friends. And if they are the same people who helped the Elephant and the Gorilla Tribe then we must act quickly to prepare the tribe for an attack."

⬤

The northeastern coast of The Golden Path is home to both the Bear Tribe and the Salmon Tribe. The members of both of these tribes had elected to be ruled by the traditional tribal system of chiefs instead of a king. The Bear Tribe is ruled by Chief Grawn. Chief Grawn is a chubby man of five feet eight inches with broad shoulders, light brown eyes and a deep gruff voice. He was a total dictator and could be a ruthless and vicious man. Although Chief Grawn is a sharp dresser he is somewhat of a slob when it comes to eating. There are two things Chief Grawn likes doing: eating salmon and spending time with his beautiful wife, Brighthea.

Chief Grawn has been known for killing men who have laid eyes on his wife, even some of his own friends have been put to death for looking at her. Chief Grawn's wife has been the reason for many battles. Brighthea is so exquisitely captivating that most people are instantly drawn to her, however, that is the problem. You see, Brighthea has "the curse of the sun." If you look at her for more than seven seconds your mind will play tricks on you, you will believe that she is after you, and you will stop at nothing to possess her love even to the point of sneaking to her bedside to wake her, resulting in waking the Chief who immediately executes you. In the past he has executed his own brother and many acquaintances. This curse, "The Curse of the Sun," was the result of Brighthea, who is of the Bear Tribe, being born outdoors during the hibernation period of bears.

Chief Grawn was told by his General that they were holding someone who had requested an audience with the Chief. Chief Grawn consulted his general, who said he should not because the person is a nobody. "We should probably let him go and force him to leave our tribal area at once." Chief Grawn then asked his wife if he should see what this person wanted with him. Brighthea advised, "Yes, I believe you should see this man and find out for yourself what he wants."

Chief Grawn agreed to see this person. The guard brought forth a remarkable person: over seven feet tall, dressed in a full length black robe covering black leather clothing and boots. The person told the chief he came from the west side of the old land, far away from The Golden Path. The person told the Chief, "Where we are from we adore salmon too, yet we have found a way to make our salmon much larger than the average fish."

"What do you mean?" asked the Chief, while he asked himself, "Can this be true?"

The person told him they had accomplished this by farming their fish, breeding them to be larger, than wild fish. Chief Grawn asked to see one of the fish. A fish was brought before him. The person was right: the fish was twice as large as the one in Salmon Creek.

The person told the Chief, "I would be willing to make a trade with you for the fish. If you place this fish in the creek it will mate with others and their offspring will be much larger."

Chief Grawn considered this then said to the person, "We don't even know you. Before we can do anything I would have to talk to my tribe and see what they have to say about this matter before I can make my decision. For now you will be free to do as you wish as long as you don't make any problems."

The next day the decision had been made by Chief Grawn. He decided to take one of the farmed fish and experiment. If things turned out like the unknown person said then the Chief would order more fish from this unknown person. The trade was done.

✺

The next day the Council sent out a request to meet with all of the tribes who live along The Golden Path. The meeting was to be held the next day. Every tribe's presence was required.

The next day arrived and the meeting began. First the Council welcomed all of the tribes, thanking them for showing up on such short notice. "We have a matter we need to talk about. It concerns all of us, so for now we will turn this meeting over to the Peace Keeper from Deer Street, Dar-boo."

Dar-boo said to all of the tribes, "An invader of some sort has been seen flying over the Cheetah territory. There are seven of these invaders, and they fly on the backs of seven baboons with wings." A murmur spread among the members of the group. Dar-boo gave them a moment, then continued. "First we need to hear from the Lion, Bear, and Tiger Tribes, as to what they saw at their last battle with the Elephant and Gorilla Tribes."

The Lion Tribe's general, Leo-Paul, stood and walked to the front to tell them what he had witnessed at that battle. Leo-Paul told them, "We lost that night, for the first time. Everything was going as planned, or so we thought. We attacked like we always attack—from the front and rear—but something happened to our rear. I sent my sergeant to take men over the other side of the hill and attack from the rear. All I can tell you is there was no rear to be found. When we went to look for the men who were supposed to be there, most of them were already dead. My men were laid out all over the field. There was blood everywhere and men yelling out for help. It was like nothing I have ever seen," said Leo-Paul.

"That will be all," said the Council to Leo-Paul. "You may be excused."

Dar-boo then asked to speak with someone from the Tiger Tribe. That is when Queen Nstar stood up to speak in front of the Council. Queen Nstar said to the Council, "We too, suffered a great loss in that battle with the Elephant and Gorilla Tribes. I had told one of my best warriors to tell me if he saw anything different in their tactics. He told me no, but he did see some men who were larger than the men of the Elephant and Gorilla tribe usually are."

Dar-boo said to the Council, "Next I would like to have the Bear Tribe come and tell what they saw different about that battle." Tarnym, the general of the Bear Tribe's army stood up and said to all of the other tribes, "I am representing the Bear Tribe. I myself did not notice anything unusual in the last battle."

Dar-boo asked Tarnym, "Where is Chief Grawn, and why isn't he attending this meeting?"

Tarnym replied, "He is busy, so he sent me."

Dar-boo said to all of the tribes, "We must stick together, and we must look out for another attack. All tribes on The Golden Path must come to the aid of one another for help.

Chancellor Shenot of the Hyena Tribe stood up and said to the Council, "I know that my tribe and I have not been the best friend nor someone the tribes on The Golden Path trust. However, I swear, on my tribe, we will be there for the members of The Golden Path, for we are all as one when it comes to defending our home, The Golden Path. My tribe and I will defend this with our very lives. I swear to the other tribes and to you, the Council of The Golden Path."

Chancellor Shenot also said to the Lion Tribes, "General Leo-Paul, will you please tell King Zhuan that I, Chancellor Shenot of the Hyena Tribe, must ask for his forgiveness.

"I must ask his forgiveness for the wrongdoing; the sadness I gave him when I rigged the time vessel that his daughter was on." Chancellor Shenot went on to say, "I know that it is our nature to be rivals, but I promise never to enter another man's family in a conflict again."

"This goes out to the new members of The Golden Path, the Jaguar Tribe," Chancellor Shenot said, "Welcome. I am truly grateful that your tribe lives here among the rest of the tribes of The Golden Path where you rightfully deserve to be."

Chancellor Shenot said, "To the new Prime Minister of the Jaguar Tribe. Afro-Light, as soon as you see your mother, Moo-su, tell her she is welcomed in my tribe, and tell her not to be a stranger."

Chancellor Shenot continued to speak in front of the Council and to the other tribes of The Golden Path. "There is still something that I must do, Afro-Light." Chancellor Shenot said, "This is to your beautiful wife, Nyrubi."

Nyrubi stood.

"I owe you my life. Furthermore, I plan to pay you for everything you have suffered in the past, and I ask you for your forgiveness, Nyrubi. My tribe and I will be there for the members of The Golden Path. That is my final word on the matter," Chancellor Shenot said to the other members of The Golden Path.

Nyrubi began to tell all of the tribes how glad she was to be part of The Golden Path; how she admired the respect tribes showed for each other's land, and customs. "That is what makes this land the greatest land of all.

"I would like to thank everyone who had a part in searching and finding me. Also I would like to take this opportunity to tell someone how much I love her. It is my older sister Shar-nu, who I never knew I had and also to my cousin Sebnala for their leadership and courage in finding me."

Nyrubi told the Council, "We must stick together if we are to defeat whatever comes our way. Furthermore the women of The Golden Path must take up arms. We, the women of The Golden Path, will become our own army. The person who will teach us is Afro-Light's mother, Moo-su. Moo-su will teach us all how to properly defend ourselves as women, for she is a master in the arts of self-defense. I had hoped to hear her speak today in front of you all, but maybe next time we all meet she will indeed speak."

One of the members of the Council said, "Thank you for that encouragement Nyrubi. I myself agree with you in the matter of the women taking up arms. I think that since we are all here we should vote on the matter."

They all voted yes to having a separate Women's Army, and agreed that all tribes would stick together in these perilous times. Afro-Light stood up and asked the Council if he might speak for a moment. The Council agreed to hear him.

Afro-Light told the Council, "Since The Golden Path sits inside of a crater, we should have armies stationed at strategic points all around. These lookout spots should be camouflaged so that they have a clear view of everything but they themselves cannot be detected. My tribe and I would be honored to carry out that detail."

Dar-boo said to Afro-Light. "Already your presence here on The Golden Path has proven to be a great asset and a most valuable and welcome addition to our tribes.

"We appreciate your acute awareness of our vulnerability in regard to The Golden Path's borders. The Council and I fully agree with your observation and accept your offer to carry out the task of guarding our borders."

Dar-boo told the Council, "Afro-Light's idea solves a multitude of concerns that we have had. Now we will be able to see when someone is approaching." He went on to say, "Since the Elephant Tribe always attacks from the northwest side of The Golden Path, we should put part of the Council's Army under Afro-Light's command as well, in order to secure the entire border."

Prince Amtar of the Cheetah stood up and stated, "This has been a truly historic day, which I am grateful to have witnessed; a day for all of us to remember. It takes a lot for a man or a woman to put their differences aside for the better of their land."

Then out of nowhere came a huge deep voice that said out loud, "I could not say it better myself, Prince Amtar." Everyone looked to the back of the chamber: it was King Zhuan from the Lion Tribe, with Moo-su from the Jaguar Tribe on his left. As they both started walking to the front of the chamber the tribes of The Golden Path gave them a full seven-minute standing ovation.

The Golden Path has great respect for both King Zhuan and Lady Moo-su for what they had to endure over the years past. King Zhuan thanked Dar-boo, the Council and the other tribes of The Golden Path for letting him speak with such short notice. King Zhuan told all of the tribes, "The future of our land is under attack, so we must defend it with our lives. We do not know who or what these Invaders are yet, nor what it is they want, but I do know if we all are weak then—and only then—can they defeat us."

King Zhaun continued, "Prince Amtar of the Cheetah Tribe, Chancellor Shenot of the Hyena Tribe, Prime Minister Afro-Light of the Jaguar Tribe, General Leo-Paul of the Lion Tribe. You must be strong for your people. Let them know what took place here today. Tell your people they must be prepared for battle. Furthermore, give your people some kind of signal or call, so that if they hear or see it they will prepare themselves for war on short notice. So watch out for things that do not seem right or are unusual. We may have endured great losses, but we shall prevail, for the future of The Golden Path and its children," said King Zhuan.

"I will look forward to working with you all. We are having a dinner in two weeks, and I would truly be offended if you all were not present. So for now be safe, be alert and know your surroundings. Moreover may glory be with The Golden Path."

Dar-boo said to Moo-su, "I hope you won't be upset with us for voting on a matter when you were not present, especially since the matter concerns you."

Moo-su said to Dar-boo, "Which matter is that?"

Dar-boo told Moo-su that she had been nominated to be the leader of the new Women's Army, as proposed by Nyrubi. "And we all agreed, so we voted on it. The vote was a unanimous win for you. So will you accept the new job? And if so who will you have for your second in command?"

Moo-su said, "Yes, thank you, I will indeed accept the job and for the position of my second in command of the army I select Queen Nstar."

Queen Nstar was surprised because it had been her great-grandmother, Queen Mayon, who had framed the Jaguar Tribe for killing Comboos, the first Peace Keeper. Lady Moo-su said to Queen Nstar, "I too look forward to sitting down with you and talking. What happened in the past will stay in the past, so we can go to the future."

Queen Nstar said to Moo-su, "I agree, and thank-you Moo-su."

The members of the Council stood up and asked the tribes of The Golden Path, "Is their anything else that needs to be said here at this meeting?"

"Who will tell the Bear and the Salmon Tribes?" said Shenot.

The Council said, "Prince Amtar, Dar-boo and you, Chancellor Shenot, will let the Bear and Salmon Tribes know what took place here."

◉

## THE BATTLE OF THE FISH PARTY

The next day Prince Amtar, Chancellor Shenot and the Peace Keeper Dar-boo talked over breakfast before taking the trip up to the

Salmon and Bear Tribes. Dar-boo told both men, "There are two things we all need to know: first of all we must leave after we eat, because it is time for the Salmon Creek fish party."

"What is a fish party?" asked Prince Amtar.

Dar-boo replied, "A fish party takes place when the salmon go back upstream to where they were born. The Salmon and Bear Tribes celebrate this occasion on the Salmon Creek. That is where things get a little difficult, because both tribes think the salmon in Salmon Creek are a gift from their gods so they take care of the Creek, furthermore they take the Creek very seriously. The slightest misunderstanding or problem with the Salmon Creek could start a war, so we must be careful about this matter."

"What are the leaders like?" asked Chancellor Shenot.

Dar-boo said, "They are both great leaders in their own right. Emperor Albertine of the Salmon Tribe is more understanding when it comes to reasoning with him. Emperor Albertine has a son who he thinks very highly of. Emperor Albertine feels his people should run wild with the salmon in Salmon Creek, and the Salmon Tribe spent a lot of time taking care of the creek, keeping the creek clean and fresh. Now, Chief Grawn is a totally different person than Emperor Albertine, for Chief Grawn of the Bear Tribe does not care so much about how clean the water is, as long as his people can eat all the salmon. Chief Grawn has no understanding about two things, and this is very important that you listen to what I am about to say."

Dar-boo said to the two men, "Chief Grawn is not easy on one's eye because he dresses very nicely but he is a slob when he eats. Nevertheless his wife Brighthea is one of the finest women on The Golden Path. Brighthea has the curse of the sun."

"What is that?" asked Prince Amtar.

Dar-boo replied to Prince Amtar, "If the sun is out then you cannot look at her for more than seven seconds, for you will find yourself trying to get her attention, even in front of the chief. I have heard of men who laid eyes on her and found themselves on the side of her bed trying to wake her, but sadly the only person who woke up was Chief Grawn, and he will have anyone killed for trying to talk to Brighthea."

"Which leader shall we talk to first?" Chancellor Shenot asked.

Dar-boo said, "We will visit the Salmon Tribe and Emperor Albertine, and maybe he will come with us to speak to Chief Grawn."

Dar-boo, Chancellor Shenot, Prince Amtar and their men made their way to see Chief Grawn of the Bear Tribe and Emperor Albertine of the Salmon Tribe.

⊕

The Salmon Tribe was getting ready for the fish party ceremonies.

Emperor Albertine told his people, "This year is a special year, for this year my son, Waterflow, will represent me at the ceremonies. Go, my people, to the Salmon Creek and be as one with the salmon in the creek. This year the gods have been great to us so go and thank them for what great harvest we all experienced."

Emperor Albertine said to his son, Waterflow, "Lead your people to the creek. You will be in charge of the army also, so make wise decisions and think critically about each and every situation that comes your way."

⊕

At the same time Chief Grawn of the Bear Tribe was getting his people ready for the Fish Party ceremonies. Chief Grawn would not be attending this years festivities, but his wife Brighthea and her cousin Keema would be attending the ceremonies with his people, and his army. Keema was a woman with the gift of hospitality: she could make the unknown person feel at home.

The Salmon Creek splits the Bear and Salmon Tribes' territories The Bear Tribe is on the west side of the creek and the Salmon Tribe is on the east side.

The Salmon Tribe arrived at the creek first and began their ceremonies. That's when one of the men of the Salmon Tribe army noticed something going on, on the other side of the creek. He reported it to an army officer, who took it to his commander, General Tex.

General Tex asked Waterflow to join him as he and men from his army went to take a closer look. When they got down to the creek they, Waterflow and General Tex saw someone they had never seen before. It was the unknown person; the same person who had made the trade with the Bear Tribe. He appeared to be preparing to release a fish into the creek, a strange, malformed fish.

Waterflow, General Tex and a few of the men from the army crossed the creek to confront the stranger. Waterflow approached and said, "Stop! Do not put that sickly looking fish—or whatever you call that—in this creek. If you put that fish in the creek you will give me no choice but to place you under arrest."

The unknown person looked up at Waterflow and began speaking, but his voice was nothing Waterflow or the General had ever heard before. It was like he was talking with the wind.

The General looked up to the sky and before he knew what had happened he, Waterflow and the army were under attack from the sky. The Salmon Tribe never knew what hit them. When the rest of the Salmon Tribe arrived all they saw was the men of their tribe dead, and their creek red with blood. The people of the Salmon rushed to the creek.

One of the sergeants of the army, Sergeant Carlay, was the first to realize Waterflow was not among the dead. He yelled out loudly, "Waterflow! We must find Waterflow!" There was a mad search to find Waterflow, the future Emperor of the Salmon Tribe, but to no avail.

There was talk the tears, "How could this have happened?" "Who could do something so outrageous; showing no respect for another man?" "The Bear Tribe did this! They have wanted to do away with us forever."

Sergeant Carlay told twelve of his men to come with him and ordered the rest of the men of the army to get their people home safely, to secure the Emperor, and to tell all the warriors to get ready to attack the Bear Tribe, or whoever proved responsible for the massacre.

Sergeant Carlay said, "We will find who did this and make them pay with their lives. Go home and be safe."

●

As Sergeant Carlay rode off with his men to look for Waterflow, Emperor Albertine was in his quarters enjoying dinner with some of the leaders of his tribe. They were interrupted by a member of the army, who entered the Emperor's quarters quite out of breath. One of the men dining with the Emperor said, "What is wrong? What has happened?" And the man who was at the creek began telling the leaders and the Emperor what had happened at the creek.

One of the leader asked, "Did you see this enemy?"

"I saw nothing, sir. It happened so fast no one knows. All I do know is that as we approached the creek, Waterflow and General Tex saw something they went to investigate. They told us to remain where we were. When they did not return we decided to go see what could have taken them so long. All we saw was a creek full of blood with our men floating in the creek."

The soldier went on , "I am sorry to report this, but we did not find Waterflow, or his body. We do not know if he is alive or dead."

Emperor Albertine stood up and said, "Someone has murdered my son! Let it be known, there is nowhere these villains will be able to hide. There is no place I will not travel, no one I will not kill in order to find the murderer of my son and my people." And to himself he thought, "There is only one rival I can think of: the Bear Tribe. They have long been a rival of ours, but I have never thought they could resort to such a thing as this. Yet, I cannot get it out of my mind that it might well be the Bear Tribe."

Emperor Albertine told the soldier, "Rise up, for you are now a sergeant of my army. Go and prepare for war. We will attack at dawn."

Then Emperor Albertine looked at his leaders and said, "I personally will lead my army in this campaign of war against the Bear Tribe, which I think must be responsible for this massacre. All of you officers, ready your elite warriors for war. Longair, you remain awhile longer."

"Yes, Emperor," they chorused, and all but Longair left the Emperor's quarters.

Emperor Albertine asked Longair if attacking the Bear Tribe before talking to Chief Grawn about what happened at the creek would be wrong.

Leader Longair said to the Emperor, "It had to be the Bear Tribe. Who else could be at the Fish Party at the same time as us? But Emperor Albertine you are the leader of this tribe, and only you can make that decision for the Salmon Tribe. Whatever you decide we your people shall back you fully."

Emperor Albertine said, "I will miss my son greatly. I must do this for my people who were murdered at the creek, and for that I say it must be war with the Bear Tribe at once."

※

When Dar-boo, Prince Amtar and Chancellor Shenot reached the Salmon Tribe territory they saw everyone carrying weapons and forming lines, as if they were ready to march off to war in a moment. Dar-boo and the others hurried to meet the Emperor. Emperor Albertine greeted them.

"Dar-boo, I am glad to see you all. It has been a long time, but you must forgive me now. This is a sorrowful day. I am about to march my people to war against the Bear Tribe, which has attacked my people and killed my son."

Dar-boo expressed his sympathy, asking Emperor Albertine to provide him more information. Since Dar-boo was Peace Keeper, Emperor Albertine consented and stopped long enough to tell Dar-boo, Prince Amtar and Chancellor Shenot what had happened at the Fish Party.

Dar-boo replied, "My friend, on our way up to see you we saw the Bear Tribe starting their own territory party. I do not think they would take the time out from their Fish Party to launch an attack. How do you know that it was the Bear Tribe? I understand your sorrow, but for the safety of your people you must be absolutely certain it was them before you attack." Dar-boo also told Emperor Albertine, "Let us tell you about the Council meeting. They requested that everyone attend but since you did not, we were chosen by the Council to inform you of what was discovered."

Chancellor Shenot told Emperor Albertine, "There have been some unknown things in the sky. The Council and the members of The Golden Path call them The Invaders."

Prince Amtar said, "We suspect them of being behind the last attack on the Lion, Tiger and Bear Tribes."

"Why is that?" Emperor Albertine asked.

"Because the three Golden Path tribes have never lost to the Elephant or Gorilla Tribes in a battle before, so they had to have something or someone to help them when they attacked The Golden Path last time."

Dar-boo asked Emperor Albertine if he could wait to go to war until they spoke with Chief Grawn of the Bear Tribe. "Give us two days to find out who is responsible for the murders at the creek."

Emperor Albertine replied, "I will try to keep my people calm, but I will not stop Sergeant Carly from looking for my son, Waterflow, and any other people who might have survived the killings. Moreover I will not stop the ones who feel they must go out and avenge their loved ones."

Prince Amtar said to Emperor Albertine, "To let your people go out for revenge without a plan is suicide for the rest of your people. Please let us find out if it was the Bear, Elephant or Gorilla Tribes, or The Invaders."

Emperor Albertine said to Prince Amtar, "I will give you two days, but if you are not back with some kind of answer then I will launch a massive attack on the Bear Tribe—one like you or I have never ever seen on another tribe who lives among The Golden Path before."

Chancellor Shenot told Emperor Albertine, "This is what we spoke about at the meeting. We have all agreed to stick together, and that is what we must do in this matter. We must trust each other, and not let any outsider tear us apart, because if we fight amongst ourselves we will surely lose everything we worked so hard to get."

Emperor Albertine said to Dar-boo, "I am not thinking right at this moment. I would like to thank you for being here at this particular time and for having this talk with me, Dar-boo, Prince Amtar, and Chancellor Shenot. I shall give you the two days you have requested. If I do not hear from any of you within two days then I will launch the attack against the Bear Tribe."

Dar-boo thanked Emperor Albertine for the time he had granted them, knowing they had done as much as they could and there was no time to be wasted. The three departed immediately for the Bear Tribe's territory.

Dar-boo reminded Prince Amtar and Chancellor Shenot, "Remember, when we go to talk to Chief Grawn do not look at his wife Brighthea, for she is plagued by the ancient curse of the sun."

❂

Brighthea and her cousin Keema were deep in conversation as they walked home from the Fish Party. Keema was telling Brighthea how the unknown person and herself had become good friends. "He would like to see me again," she giggled.

"What did you tell him?" Brighthea asked Keema.

Keema replied, "I told him I would meet him after the Fish Party ceremonies, so that is where I must go now. Cousin Brighthea, I shall tell you everything about him when I return."

Brighthea quickly asked, "Keema what is his name?"

Keema said, "He told me it was Hardstone. I must go now."

❂

Brighthea returned with her people from the Fish Party ceremonies and noticed immediately that her husband, Chief Grawn, had visitors. Chief Grawn introduced her to Dar-boo, Prince Amtar and Chancellor Shenot.

Chief Grawn invited his wife to have a seat beside him, and Brighthea did so as the four men began to talk.

Prince Amtar said to Chief Grawn, "We first came to let you know what was said at the Council meeting we had the other day, but sadly now we have some bad news to tell you."

"What bad news?" Chief Grawn asked.

Chancellor Shenot began telling the Chief what had happened the day before. "Some of the Salmon Tribe's men were attacked yesterday. Emperor Albertine and his people think it was your tribe who attacked them."

Dar-boo asked Chief Grawn if he knew of an attack that had taken place the day before.

Chief Grawn answered, "No, we the Bear Tribe have been at the Fish Party ceremonies for the last two days. And I would not launch an attack on another tribe who lives on The Golden Path before going to see the Council."

"Emperor Albertine lost his son Waterflow yesterday in the attack. If there is anything you know you should tell us," said Prince Amtar.

"My tribe would not do such a cowardly thing as that! It would not be the actions a true warrior." Chief Grawn asked Dar-boo, "What was said at the Council meeting? It had to be of some importance for you three to come and speak with me."

Chancellor Shenot spoke. "Yes, it is important for you to know what was said at the Council meeting. All of the tribes have agreed that we have some outsider, or unknown person among us who will try to destroy us if we let them. So far we've only seen seven of these outsiders. The members of The Golden Path have named them The Invaders.

"The Invaders attack from the sky, for they ride on the backs of seven baboons with wings."

Dar-boo picked up the conversation. "We suspect The Invaders will try and start a war between the tribes of The Golden Path because it will be much easier for them to take over The Golden Path if we are fighting each other."

Dar-boo continued, "The Higher Power has always been at our side; when our children were born or when we marched off to war. Yet the last battle we had against the Elephant and the Gorilla Tribe a lot of our tribes suffered defeat. Your tribe was there but for some reason you did not lose a lot of men."

Chief Grawn replied, "We were there with the Lion and Tiger Tribes, and I did not notice anything different about the Gorilla or the Elephant Tribe that would make me be alarmed. Furthermore, if I did I would have alerted all of the tribes among The Golden Path."

Prince Amtar asked again, "Chief Grawn, have you seen or heard of anything going on differently?"

Chief Grawn looked at Brighthea, then said to Prince Amtar, "There was a man who came in front of me the other day. The unknown man told me he was from the west side of the old land and his people there enjoy fish just as much as we do. Then he asked me if I would look at his people's salmon, for their fish are larger than the fish we have in Salmon Creek."

"What did you do?" asked Chancellor Shenot.

Chief Grawn replied, "I told the unknown person if he would leave one of his farm fish my people would look at it, and that if they approve the fish then I will try one. And so I did. I regret I let him put the fish he had in the creek."

"Where is this man?" asked Dar-boo.

Chief Grawn answered, "I do not know where he is at the moment."

That is when Lady Brighthea asked her husband if she could speak. Chief Grawn answered yes, and Brighthea began speaking to the men. "My cousin, Keema, told me she was going to meet with the unknown person. She also told me his name ... if I could remember.

"Oh yes, forgive me, His name was Hardstone."

"Where is Keema now, Brighthea?" asked Dar-boo the Peace Keeper who kept his head toward her husband.

"I cannot tell you for I do not know myself. But I can assure you as soon as I see her I will bring her here."

Chief Grawn promised Dar-boo he would get to the bottom of the questions about the stranger. "Furthermore, I would be honored if you all—Dar-boo, Prince Amtar, and Chancellor Shenot—would stay as our guests and have dinner with my wife and her cousin, Keema."

"Thank you, Chief Grawn," said Dar-boo, who accepted the invitation.

❖

As the day turned to night Keema found herself enjoying her time with the stranger, Hardstone. Keema asked, "Your land where you are from, the west side of the old land, why do your people farm their fish instead of letting mother nature take place, so the fish could be free and wild the way they should be?"

Hardstone looked at Keema and began telling her how his people sell their fish to people in the real world. Hardstone continues when they both realized they were out of the Bear Territory. "The better the product, and the more it weighs, the faster we can get the product to the consumer, the faster the company will grow."

Keema said, "So if you farm the fish you can breed them faster. I understand."

Keema said to Hardstone, "I have enjoyed this time we have spent together and I hope and look forward to the next time we meet. Now I must go, I have a dinner engagement with Chief Grawn and my cousin Brighthea."

As Keema began to walk away Hardstone grabbed her and said, "I am sorry Keema but I cannot let you go."

Keema said to Hardstone, "I demand you release me at once!" Keema began to scream at Hardstone.

Hardstone said, "I know that you do not understand, but in time you will come to see that I am doing this for your own good. I do not want to hurt you Keema, but for now you must come with me."

He made sure he had a secure grip on her as he began calling out to the wind.

Keema looked at Hardstone as if he was from a planet other than The Land of The Seven. She asked him what he said. Before he could say another word to her the wind began to blow, and right before Keema's eyes something landed on the ground. Keema was horrified. The thing was looking directly at her. It opened its mouth and growled at her. All she could see was two front canine teeth that were as big as she was. It must have been at least twenty feet tall! But what startled her most was that it had wings. The thing could fly! It was one of those huge Baboons that the Invaders ride on. Hardstone grabbed Keema and with one swift motion they were on the back of the flying Baboon. Hardstone told Keema to hold on as they flew out into the darkness.

●

Back at the Bear Tribe Dar-boo, Chancellor Shenot, and Prince Amtar were preparing themselves for dinner in the guest quarters. Prince Amtar told the other two men, "All we have to do is talk to Keema tonight at dinner."

"How do we know if she will tell us anything?" said Chancellor Shenot. This stranger who calls himself Hardstone may not tell Keema anything at all."

It was time for the feast and everyone at Chief Grawn's table was seated except for Keema.

Chief Grawn asked Brighthea, "Where is Keema?"

Brighthea replied, "She told me she was going to meet with Hardstone, but I am sure she knows about the dinner we are having tonight. She seemed eager to talk to the Peace Keeper Dar-boo about The Golden Path's past."

Brighthea called one of her servants. "Go find Keema and bring her to the Chief's table at once."

Chief Grawn told two of his men to assist the servants in the search to look for Keema.

Quite a bit of time had passed when both the servant and the two men came in front of the Chief with bad news: there was no trace of Keema.

Chief Grawn's first thought was that the disappearance of Keema was the doing of the Salmon Tribe, but Dar-boo, Chancellor Shenot, and Prince Amtar assured Chief Grawn that Emperor Albertine had given his word he would not attack. "He would wait until we spoke with him or two days if we did not return. We are sure you can rule out the Salmon Tribe."

Chancellor Shenot said to Dar-boo, "We must send our men to find this Hardstone as soon as possible. We mustn't give whoever has Keema a lot of time, and I think we all agree it is probably this man who has taken her away."

Chief Grawn said, "No, I will send my men. If it is Hardstone who is behind this then I think it would be best if you three go warn Emperor Albertine and his tribe about this Invader. Tell him the Bear Tribe would not bring harm his way at any time, but for now it will take both of our tribes' intelligence to defeat these Invaders."

Hardstone had taken Keema to a hideout. It was a water cave. Keema had never seen a water cave, and the beauty of it made her mind wander off the thought of being kidnapped for just a moment.

Hardstone was watching Keema, and she asked him, "Just why are you doing this to me? I have not offended you in any way."

Hardstone replied, "You have asked me two questions. For now I will answer only one. You asked me who I am, and I will tell you. There are seven of us and we are 'game hunters.' We follow game wherever it might go. When we stumbled across your land we said to each other, 'We must have it.'"

Keema then asked Hardstone, "Then who is the game?"

Hardstone replied, "You mean who is the 'hunted'? That, dear lady, would be the men of The Golden Path."

Hardstone went on to tell Keema more about the game hunters, ending with, "The other six game hunters are full game hunters, but I am part man and part game hunter." Hardstone paused. "I have told you who I really am, and now I must go and prepare for war. I will not tie you up, but if you give me one reason then I shall."

Hardstone walked to the front of the water cave to speak with the rest of the game hunters. He began speaking to the them in their "wind" language. "Go and alert the Elephant and the Gorilla Tribes. Tell them to get in position to attack the Bear and the Salmon Tribes. They are to march to the outside of the Bear and Salmon Tribes territories, but wait for my call to attack." The game hunters then flew away on the backs of the baboons with wings.

Several minutes passed before Keema realized she was alone in the water cave. She began walking around, amazed at what she saw. She had heard of the place called the "Cave of One Hundred Waterfalls," but now she was actually inside of it.

As Keema was exploring the water cave and its lovely waterfalls she became aware of an unusual sound. At first she had thought it was just the water from the waterfalls hitting the rocks below, but now she realized it was something different. As Keema approached the waterfall where she had heard the noises the noises became louder and louder.

Keema looked into the water and immediately jumped back because what she saw frightened her. It was two men behind the waterfall, and they were tied up. Keema went behind the waterfall where the two men were being held hostage. She took the bandages off of their mouths and whispered to them asking who they were.

One man said, "I am Waterflow, son of the Great Emperor Albertine of the Salmon Tribe. This man is my army's highest general, General Tex. We were abducted fom the Fish Party and taken hostage by whatever you call those things."

Waterflow asked, "What is your name?"

"Keema from the Bear Tribe. I am also being held against my will by the leader of the Invaders. They are called 'game hunters,' and his name is Hardstone."

Keema said to Waterflow, "I must return to where he left me, but I will untie you both. I will also find out the game hunters' plan."

Keema also said to the two men, I" notice the other game hunters could not fit into the entrance of the cave, so when Hardstone returns to check on you, the two of you must attack him."

"What about the others?" said Waterflow.

General Tex said we would handle them.

Keema told the two men, "I must go now before Hardstone returns, so goodbye for now."

✺

Sergeant Carlay and his men felt they were getting closer to where their chief's son, Waterflow, was being held. Carlay had told his men they would not return to their homeland without rescuing Waterflow or recovering his dead body. Sergeant Carlay and his men were now in the southeast section of The Golden Path near the border of the Hyena Tribe's territory. There was only one remaining place they had not searched, and that was the treacherous region that sheltered the ancient water caves. Those water caves separated the Old Land from The Golden Path. They had been the route by which tribes of the Old Land had moved to The Golden Path. Sergeant Carly knew there were many people who had not crossed the water caves, but had stayed within them. He knew they would be moving about the falls trying not to be seen by anyone. And he knew that if there were discovered things could get out of hand.

✺

Assembled at the Salmon Tribe with Emperor Albertine were the ruling parties of The Golden Path. In attendance was Dar-boo, Chancellor Shenot, Prince Amtar and even Chief Grawn, who was making his first appearance on that side of the creek.

Dar-boo announced to Emperor Albertine, "Someone wants to speak with you." And then he stepped aside.

Chief Grawn of the Bear Tribe walked up to Emperor Albertine of the Salmon Tribe, and said, "I am facing you to let you know that my tribe had nothing to do with the disappearance of your son, Waterflow, or the killing of your people. He continued, saying, "It has been discovered that your tribe and mine are the focus of an elaborate plan to manipulate us into going into war with each other. Yes, we have allowed these Invaders to do damage to our people. So I say to you Emperor Albertine, we must work together and investigate this matter. I have already dispatched my top warriors to assist your Sergeant Carlay in the search and rescue of your son. We must seek out these Invaders. They are the masterminds behind all of this, and we do not know the full extent of their intentions.

Dar-boo said to everyone, "I will send a message to the Council and to the rest of the tribes, telling them to be on alert and ready to aid us if needed."

The next day the messenger arrived at the Lion Tribe's territory where all of the leaders of the other tribes and the Council of The Golden Path were having dinner. The messenger was immediately taken to King Zhuan of the Lion Tribe. King Zhuan opened the message. After reading it he called for everyone's full attention. Then he said, "It is from Dar-boo. He writes to inform us that the Invaders have kidnapped Keema, the cousin of Chief Grawn's wife, and they have killed the son of Emperor Albertine, Waterflow. Both the Bear Tribe and the Salmon Tribes have prepared for war against the Elephant and Gorilla Tribes. He has reason to believe the Invader will be among them when they attack."

Upon hearing this, the leaders agreed that between the two tribes there were enough men to defend themselves; however, they decided their mission would be to destroy the opposition completely. For this they would need one more tribe to defend the northeast side of The Golden Path. They could send General Leo-Paul of the Lion Tribe or Afro-Light, Prime Minister of the Jaguar Tribe to help defeat the Gorilla and Elephant Tribe once and for all.

King Zhuan looked at everyone at his royal table then at Leo-Pau, then he said, "Go and alert your army that you shall leave at once to participate in the defeat of these pests."

Afro-Light said to everyone at the royal table, "My army shall go with you Leo-Paul."

The Council said, "No. The Golden Path needs to be protected on the west side also. Leo-Paul and Afro-Light make sure you have this side covered against an attack. We, the Council's Army, will go assess Dar-boo the Peace Keeper and the others. That will give us an extra tribe to defend this side."

King Zhuan said, "Afro-Light you must go and tell Graceshell of the Cheetah Tribe and Mark, the son of Chancellor Shenot, to prepare and guard the borders of their tribes. They must lead their tribe while the Council leaders are assisting the Bear and Salmon Tribes in the final war against the Elephant and Gorilla Tribes. Tell them they must be the leader they are supposed to be and that King Zhuan and rest of the tribes of The Golden Path will be there for them. They must defend the west side of The Golden Path with their lives."

King Zhuan said to Leo-Paul and Afro-Light, "I feel I should assemble my Royal Army."

Leo-Paul said, "No, my King, you have seen enough wars in your lifetime. Leave it up to us, for it is our generation's turn to defend The Golden Path, and we will not let The Golden Path, nor you down."

King Zhuan said to Afro-Light and Leo-Paul, "May the High Power be with us all as we face a new enemy. It will take everything you have learned here on The Golden Path."

"Attack the Elephant Tribe from the side said the King to Afro-Light. "Then, Leo-Paul, take your tribe and attack from the rear. They will try to use their quickness against the strength of your tribes. But this time we will have a surprise. Have a fleet of your men in the Wood Hills. Get them up into the treetops, so if they attack from the sky we will have the advantage of surprise and counter their attack more efficiently."

"Go, Afro-Light and Leo-Paul to prepare your armies for war," said King Zhuan.

Hardstone returned to the water cave and found Keema right where he had left her. Hardstone spoke to the other Game Hunters, "Take this message to the leader of the Elephant and Gorilla Tribes. Have them deliver it to Chief Grawn and Emperor Albertine." The message read simply:

> If you wish to see Waterflow or Keema again you must immediately forfeit your land to me You will not be asked a second time. If you do not comply your people will suffer the wrath of the Game Hunters.
>
> ~Hardstone,
> Leader of the Game Hunters

A little while later, back at the Salmon Tribe, twenty guards rushed into Emperor Albertine's Quarters where Chancellor Shenot, Prince Amtar, Dar-boo, and Emperor Albertine were discussing battle plans.

"The Elephant and Gorilla Tribes have begun the attack. Our front line is holding up very well, but we've lost a lot of men."

"Sir," the guard said, "I have a message for you. One of the Invaders flew over and dropped the body of one of our men. His head was cut off and this message was stuck to his back. It said to give it to our leader."

All of the leaders read the message and agreed that no one regardless of their standing was worth the lives of so many.

Emperor Albertine said, "We will not jeopardize the entire population of The Golden Path for my son or anyone's son."

Chief Grawn agreed, as did all the others.

Dar-boo said, "We must depart. Our first front will soon weaken and begin to draw on the reserves in the Wood Hills. We mustn't give our enemies any time, for the trap will only be successful if it is a surprise.:

Emperor Albertine told his guards to leave at once, to tell the men on the front line that backup was on the way, and to fight on.

◉

While the Elephant and the Gorilla Tribe with the help of the Game Hunters had begun the brutal attack against the Bear and Salmon Tribe, Hardstone remained at the water cave with Keema, Waterflow and General Tex.

Keema said to Hardstone, "You have told me your first plan. What is your second plan?"

Hardstone began telling her as he walked toward the waterfall where Waterflow and General Tex were being held. "We, the Game Hunters, will do away with the men of The Golden Path in order to take control of their women. It is top priority for us the Game Hunters to pass on our seed any way we can. There are only seven of us left, and if we want to survive and in order to make it to the next generation we must mate with as many females as possible."

Keema asked Hardstone, "So when you say do away with all of the men, you also mean my Chief?"

"Yes, even your Chief. I would like to spare him, for he is the one who let us in so we could get our plan started, but I cannot." Hardstone said this standing in front of the waterfall where Waterflow and General Tex were being held.

Keema was willing to put her life on the line to destroy Hardstone and his plans.

Hardstone walked up to Waterflow and removed the bandage from his mouth. "When the other Game Hunters return we will know whether you two live or die. It is up to the leaders of your tribes."

Waterflow said to Hardstone, "The Golden Path will not negotiate with outsiders such as yourself. You might as well kill us now, for you will not receive any answer from our leaders on that issue."

General Tex tried to say something though his mouth was gagged.

Hardstone snatched off the gag and said to him, "What did you say?"

General Tex said to Hardstone, "I need to go and relieve myself."

Hardstone said to General Tex, "I will allow it; however, don't even think about trying to escape, because if you do I will kill you both."

Keema walked back to where the men were. Hardstone ordered Keema to leave.

Keema asked, "Who are these men, Hardstone?"

He gruffly replied, "That is none of your concern. Leave from here at once!"

Without any warning Keema shouted, "NOW!"

Waterflow and General Tex began attacking Hardstone. The fight went on until Waterflow and General Tex were injured in the attack. Hardstone was injured as well but then he began laughing and bragging to them, saying, "No man can kill a Game Hunter. Now I must kill you both for your pitiful attempt to kill me."

Just as Hardstone was going to strike Waterflow with his sword, Keema picked up a sharp cone that had fallen from the top of the cave and drove it into the Hardstone's heart.

As Hardstone fell to the ground on his knees, Keema said to him, "You distinctly said 'no man' could kill you and the other Game Hunters. You never once said anything about a woman."

Hardstone looked up at Keema and with his last breath said to her, "It is too late. You will never stop the plan that is already in motion."

●

Keema told Waterflow and General Tex, "The other Game Hunters will be back soon. They cannot fit into the entrance of the water cave so if we choose to stay here we will be safe."

General Tex said to Keema and Waterflow, "We must get back to our tribes to let them know we are alright. Furthermore we must tell them not to negotiate with the Elephant and Gorilla Tribes. If our tribes know that we are alive then they will fight harder to defeat the outsiders. We must get the other Game Hungers into the cave and handle this like we did with Hardstone."

"How would we do that?" said Keema.

General Tex replied, "If they cannot fit in then we will make them fit. We will put Hardstone's body in front of the entrance and let them see it. They will try to get to his dead body, and that is when we will attack them. There should only be six of the Game Hunters left."

Keema said, "I am ready to fight to the end of my life, but I must put what took place here tonight on the wall of the water cave for future generations to remember. They will know that we defeated the Invaders called Game Hunters by sticking together for the greater cause."

Waterflow placed Hardstone's dead body in front of the water cave just enough so the other Game Hunters could see Hardstone but could not quite reach him. Keema, Waterflow, and General Tex waited for the other Game Hunters to return. Finally Waterflow heard the wind churn, and he knew that the other Game Hunters were nearly there.

General Tex said to Keema and Waterflow, "Prepare yourselves for attack."

The Game Hunters returned from the front line of the war against the Bear and Salmon Tribes. When they had all landed one of them came to the front of the cave and began to speak in their tongue. Then the wind began to rush into the cave. Suddenly it was silent.

Waterflow said to both Keema and General Tex, "Hold tight."

Then they witnessed the most chilling scene. The cave began to rumble and shake violently as the remaining six Game Hunters began making ear splitting, high pitched, piercing screaming noises and frantically began clawing and fighting their way into the cave to retrieve Hardstone's body.

Keema again yelled, "NOW!"

She was the first to attack the Game Hunter followed by both General Tex, and Waterflow.

The fight was to the death, especially for Keema, Waterflow, and General Tex. Rocks from the ceiling of the cave were falling everywhere, Keema yelled, "This is for The Golden Path!" as she fought on. It was beginning to look like Keema and the others were being overpowered, when a Game Hunter was hit by a fallen rock that trapped him. Keema ran under him and was shielded from the debris as it fell. The other Game Hunters began making their way into the cave.

The three members of The Golden Path were experienced warriors and were prepared to fight to the death as the remaining Game Hunters came closer and closer. General Tex, Keema and Waterflow looked at each other as if they felt it would be for the last time.

Waterflow yelled out, "CHARGE!" as they begin a fierce fight with the Game Hunters. The members of The Golden Path fought until it seemed they could not go on. Just as they were beginning to fear they would be defeated they started hearing the Game Hunters screaming and yelling as if they were being attacked from behind. General Tex told Keema and Waterflow to retreat into the back of the water cave. Once they safely reached the back of the cave they turned around and saw that the screaming, agonizing Game Hunters were flying away. For a brief moment it was silent and then out of nowhere Sergeant Carlay and his men began shouting for Waterflow.

Waterflow ran out to Sergeant Carlay and hugged him as the others were also greeted. Sergeant Carlay and Waterflow spoke for a moment then Sergeant Carlay asked General Tex, "Who might this woman be?"

Keema interrupted General Tex and spoke directly to the Sergeant saying, "My name is Keema from the Bear Tribe. Who would you be?"

"I am Carlay, Sergeant of the Salmon Tribe's powerful army."

Sergeant Carlay said to General Tex, "Sir we must go immediately and assess the war against both of our tribes. They will be greatly relieved to know that the two of you are alive and well. My men and I will bring up the rear, Sergeant Carlay, while you and your men lead. Waterflow and Keema are to be secured in between the two of us, just in case we get an unexpected attack."

General Tex, Sergeant Carlay and their men departed to confirm it was safe for them to make their way back to their tribes.

# THE PUSH AT COTTENBERG

The remaining Game Hunters along with the Gorilla and Elephant tribes had begun pushing the tribes of The Golden Path back into the middle of Cottenberg

It took one day for Waterflow and the others to return to the Salmon Tribe from the water caves. They found the Bear and Salmon Tribes under fierce attack.

Chief Grawn and Emperor Albertine were both delighted to see their missing family members returned to them alive and well.

General Tex said to the Emperor, "I am truly sorry for what happened to your son Waterflow. I understand I have dishonored my people and you my Emperor. I stand ready to accept my fate for my disgrace; however I do have one request. Please allow me to first go to the frontline and help my comrades in this sickly war of death."

Waterflow and Keema said to their leaders, "If General Tex and Sergeant Carlay return to the front line so shall we."

The leaders were in agreement that they, being Title Holders, were not obligated to be in combat.

Keema said, "We must."

Chief Grawn of the Bear Tribe said to General Tex, "The Peace Keeper Dar-boo sent word to us that they were in need of one more tribe to ensure their victory on the eastern side where the town of Cottenberg and the village of Michelgray are located. The other tribes will not deviate from their original orders to have the west coast prepared in case of an unexpected attack."

Waterflow asked Chief Grawn, "Will that be enough men to defeat the Outsiders?"

Emperor Albertine replied, "It will have to be enough."

General Tex told his Emperor, "We must go to the front line immediately."

After the others were dismissed, Chief Grawn and Emperor Albertine again went over Dar-boo's message. Emperor Albertine was most pleased with the portion of the message that cited Prince Amtar, Chancellor Shenot and Dar-boo were at the Battle of Cottenberg. The message from Dar-boo went on to say, "We are finally pushing the

Outsider outward for the first time in the war. The Bear and Salmon Tribes have been turning the tide against the Outsiders on the lower north side near the village of Michelgray. I know we can defeat the outsiders if we have just one more tribe. My request is that you send one of the tribes from the west side to come north to assist us."

Chief Grawn looked at Keema and the others and said, "You are most needed in the town of Cottenberg. Go, and be safe. When you see Dar-boo tell him the Council has dispatched its Superior Warriors to assist them and they should be there at any moment. So hold the frontline with whatever it takes."

# THE BATTLE OF MICHELGRAY VILLAGE

The battle of Michelgray Village was the most important battle for the members of The Golden Path to win because Michelgray provides direct access to the creek. If the outsiders controlled the village of Michelgray then they would have full control of The Golden Path's water supply. So both Chiefs put their best forces in the lower north side near Michelgray. There the members of The Golden Path could also make use of the Wood Hills.

The people of the village of Michelgray are very loyal to the tribes of The Golden Path, for they have been doing business with each other for over fifty years. The village of Michelgray provides fresh produce from their gardens and The Golden Path supplies them with fish, game and protection.

The battle at the Michelgray was also one of the most deadly battles. The tribes on both sides fought fearlessly for seven days. The loss of life was tremendous but the tide finally turned in favor of the tribes of The Golden Path when the villagers decided to enter the war and come to the aid of the Bear Tribe and the Salmon Tribe.

Villagers sent a fake message that was intercepted by the Gorilla and Elephant Tribe. It said, "The Bear and Salmon Tribes will be at the village dinner in Michelgray, so we need to triple our order for alcohol that night." The Elephant and Gorilla Tribes thought that would be a great time to invade Michelgray.

When the Gorilla and Elephant Tribes entered the village of Michelgray they were expecting some resistance from the villagers but a quick and deadly resolution. They figured they would easily conquer the Bear and Salmon Tribes by launching a surprise attack on them as they partied. They also looked forward to getting plenty of food, water and rest once the battle was won. To their great surprise the village was completely empty. The Gorilla and Elephant Tribes had been fooled into thinking they would surprise the Bear and Salmon Tribes, but instead they were the ones surprised. The Bear and Salmon Tribes had directed the villagers to move all of their food, water and livestock to the Wood Hills, so when the Gorilla and Elephant Tribes entered into the village of Michelgray they expected necessities, but there were none.

The Bear and Salmon Tribes saw that the Elephant and Gorilla Tribes were showing signs of starvation, and so they attacked. The battle was over quickly.

The decision of the armies of The Golden Path was to take prisoners of war. One of the original rules of combat was that tribes of The Golden Path would not torture or kill any of their prisoners. Dar-boo said to The Golden Path leaders, "We shall show decency to the prisoners. Our enemies are called to do the same with their P.O.W.'s. We must set the standard for conduct even in war. And so it is written."

✺

## THE LAST BATTLE

The citizens of the town of Cottenberg and the Salmon Tribe have a very tragic past in the Real World. The Salmon Tribe has attacked the town of Cottenberg many times in retaliation for the holocaust that took place in the history of these two different tribes and towns. Emperor Albertine remembers his people were murdered by the people of Cottenberg's ancestors in the Real World. Once the Salmon Tribe grew much stronger and powerful than the people of Cottonburg, Emperor Albertine made a vow to the town and to his tribe that they would not come to their aid if needed. They would not help them in any way. That is why Emperor Albertine put most of his army under the control of the Bear Tribe and Chief Grawn, since they would be fighting in Michelgray not Cottenberg.

The town of Cottenberg trades with the tribes of The Golden Path, marketing its natural resources, which include hemp and pearls. Cottenberg sells and trades hemp that they have been growing for over 200 years, from seeds passed down from generation to generation. In exchange the tribes of The Golden Path provide the town of Cottenberg with fish and produce. They use the hemp to make clothes for their army, or for other things. Cottenberg is also favorite vacation spot for the tribes on the East Coast of The Golden Path.

Chief Grawn put two of his army divisions under Dar-boo's control. Keema, Waterflow, General Tex, Sergeant Carlay, Dar-boo, Prince Amtar and Chancellor Shenot with their 200,000 men held off the invasion lead by the Game Hunters, the Elephant Tribe and the Gorilla Tribe. The Outsiders had occupied most of the town of Cottenberg so Dar-boo and the others waited silently out in the Wood Hills. Dar-boo and the others felt they would wait for dawn to attack for the final and last time. The last push to gain control of Cottenberg was long and costly for the members of The Golden Path, yet they continued to fight on until their last breath. It looked like it was going to be another defeat for The Golden Path, and that they would lose control of the town. Losing Cottenberg would be for them a vital blow.

Dar-boo and the others fought on even when they sensed defeat was near, they would not give up.

The Game Hunters and the others followed the members of The Golden Path into the Wood Hills where the members of The Golden Path could use the Wood Hills for their advantage. Dar-boo waited until the Game Hunters and the others were fully in the Wood Hills before he launched the last attack against the Elephant Tribe and the others. It was smart on the part of the members of The Golden Path because it worked in their favor. The Outsiders suffered many casualties in the Wood Hills and decided to abort their mission. When the Outsiders retreated they were in for yet another surprise. Once outside the Wood Hills they found themselves face to face with the Council's Army who had just arrived to assist the members of The Golden Path so they could do away with the Outsiders for good.

The Bear and Salmon Tribes had defeated the Outsiders down on the lower side of the little village of Michelgray. The Battle of Cottenberg was to be the final chapter of the war between the Tribes of The Golden Path and the combined band of renegades consisting of the Elephant Tribe, the Gorilla Tribe and the Game Hunters.

The Game Hunters, Gorilla and the Elephant Tribe had no choice but to surrender. It was over. The war that had begun with a simple trade had finally ended with the tribes of The Golden Path being victorious over the Gorilla Tribe, Elephant Tribe and the Game Hunters.

Chief Grawn said to both the Bear and Salmon Tribes, "We've stuck together to defeat a new enemy. I have a feeling that will not be the last time we hear or see a Game Hunter, but for now we must ten to the wounded. We will heal from this war and begin to rebui

Therefore, everyone hold your head up high! You have a lot to be proud of for your warriors and yourselves."

The Council said to the members of The Golden Path, "We will remember this day and never forget our loved ones who were lost in this War of Trade. So we the members of the Council hereby officially mark this day as O.D. Day, meaning Outsiders Defeated Day. We will be holding a meeting and all tribes must be present. This meeting will take place at the Salmon Creek where all of the tribes of The Golden Path will celebrate a real Fish Party with the Bear and Salmon Tribes.

Emperor Albertine told everyone, "Through this war we have found out just how well we would handle a surprise attack. We also saw Generals become Co-Commanders, Sergeants become Generals, and a young woman become a hero. For all that, we are truly grateful."

At the Council Meeting and the Fish Party all of the tribes were present. Dar-boo presented awards to General Tex who became Co-Commander; Sergeant Carlay, who became a General of the Salmon Tribe's army; and Keema, who became a General in the new Women's Army under the leadership of Moo-su of the Jaguar Tribe and Queen Nstar of the Tiger Tribe.

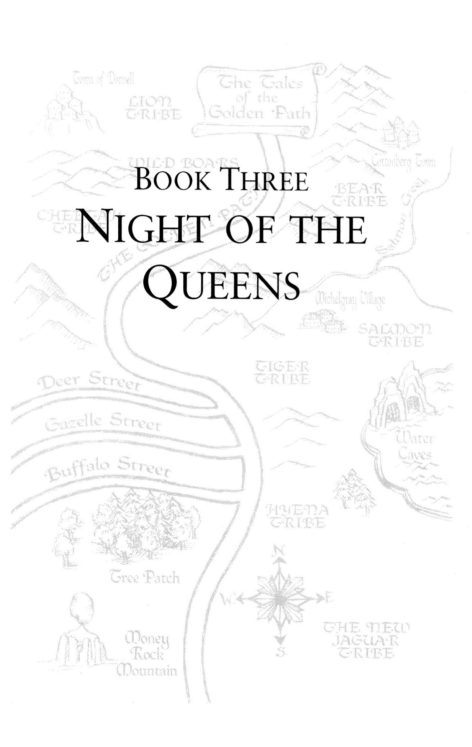

# BOOK THREE
# NIGHT OF THE
# QUEENS

# PREFACE

an the kings and queens from several different tribes learn to put aside their differences? They must come together in common cause if they are to preserve The Golden Path.

# Murder on Deer Street

O n Deer Street behind one of the betting lounges a woman has been found dead.

This is a story about Buffalo Street, Deer Street and Gazelle Street. They are commonly called "The Three Streets." In order to fund education for children both rich and poor, The Golden Path's Council had passed an ordinance allowing gambling and prostitution in the business section of The Three Streets. These activities were taxed a "suitor tax" that went to the Department of Education. Over the years the business section had become increasingly lawless, tolerating just about everything except stealing and killing.

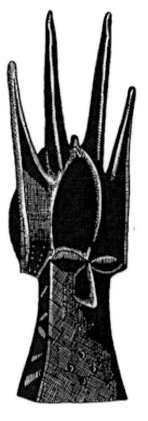

The death of the woman prompted a Council investigation, which called for all betting lounges to be shut down until the investigation was complete. This was the first killing on The Three Streets since the tribes of The Golden Path had moved there, some seventy-five years before.

The Three Streets are mostly run by the Wild Boar Tribe which considers itself to be judge, jury and executioner of The Three Streets. The other parts of The Three Streets are run by gangs. Of all the gangs that are on Buffalo Street, Deer Street and Gazelle Street, two are the most powerful and active: the Dark Rangers and the Village Daggers. Both gangs have been at war for power. They want the rights to do business with the owners of the betting lounges as well as with the Wild Boar Tribe.

Another gang has recently moved near Money Rock Mountain. They call themselves the 49er Women. These women are from the Old Land and came to The Three Streets to find gold. No one who lives on or does business on The Three Streets knows of any gold in Money Rock Mountain. The 49er Women have become rich by very discreetly and cleverly selling their gold to tribes of The Golden Path. They were determined to keep the gold in Money Rock Mountain a secret from the Wild Boar Tribe, the betting lounge owners and the gangs. Nevertheless, if the secret was to get out the 49er Women were prepared to defend Money Rock Mountain with their lives. The women feel that because they were the ones who found the gold, it is theirs for the keeping.

✠

It has been seventy-five years since the tribes moved to The Golden Path, and they will be celebrating that occasion at Karon Beach Stadium which is in the town of Darnell. This is also the year for the Title Holder Games to be held. The favorite to win this time is the Hyena Tribe, although the Cheetah Tribe is not far behind to win the Title Holder Game because of their superstar, Speed-Shay.

Speed-Shay is the daughter of Prince Amtar of the Cheetah Tribe. Speed-Shay will participate in four of the events. She is heavily favored to break the record currently held by Shar-nu of the Lion Tribe for the fastest woman on The Golden Path. The members of The Golden Path are happy and hoping Speed-Shay will break the record. The tribes of The Golden Path have been waiting to see her perform ever since she was five, and now the time has finally come to see Speed-Shay run. It's a thing of beauty.

We find Speed-Shay somewhere in the Cheetah Territory with her friend Maysheara.

Maysheara said to Speed-Shay, "You are up kind of early this morning."

Speed-Shay said to Maysheara, "Or maybe you are up too late."

As they both started laughing together, Maysheara said to Speed-Shay, "Are you ready?"

"I'm ready."

Maysheara said, "Go!"

As they began to race, it looked like Maysheara would come out the winner, but when it was all said and done, Speed-Shay ended up the winner. Both of the ladies took a seat on the side of a cliff overlooking the Cheetah Tribe's territory, as they were out of breath and exhausted from the race they just had.

Maysheara began to speak, "I am very excited about the Title Holder Games! I have been anticipating and training for this moment all my life. I even put my friendships to the side so I could put more time into my training for the Title Holder Games. I just hope that I win one Golden Hand award. It would give my tribe a better chance to officially become a member of The Golden Path."

Speed-Shay said, "Your tribe was given the right to live outside of The Three Streets."

"Yes, and that's all right. But my father is so involved in running The Three Streets that he hardly has any time for me. Don't get me wrong. It's a hard job keeping The Three Streets safe and collecting all of the taxes from every betting lounge, gambler and gang who lives or does business along The Three Streets, but that is what the Council expects and requires of my father, Prince Donshu. It is a huge responsibility and should weigh heavily in our favor when Father goes before the Council to petition them on the matter of the Wild Boar Tribe receiving their own land on The Golden Path. I believe that my father and tribe have proven that they are worthy to be members of The Golden Path. As you know my father's work environment is very dangerous. Because it is common knowledge that my father collects currency and is traveling with it to pay the Council, there is always someone waiting for him to slip so they can ambush him. I would not know what I would do if anything was to happen to my father, Speed-Shay."

Maysheara continued, "Never mind about me. What about you Speed-Shay? I know you are going to win a lot of Golden Hand awards at the Title Holder Games this year. Who can beat you except me?" And Maysheara laughed at her own joke. "But I'm serious. Who could beat you?"

Speed-Shay said, "You can, Maysheara. I know you will perform well at the Title Holder Games and you will make your tribe and your father proud of you. But Maysheara I may not compete in the Title Holder Games this year."

Maysheara said to Speed-Shay, "Whatever do you mean?"

Speed-Shay answered, "I would like to see all of The Golden Path and see how other people are from other tribes, so that is why I am going to volunteer for the new Women's Army. I have heard about the leader of the army, Moo-su, and how she raised Nyrubi from the Lion Tribe up from a little girl to a woman after Moo-su found her in a time vessel crash. I think this will give me the perfect opportunity to get to see and maybe get to know all of the great woman of The Golden Path."

♒

The next morning taxes were due from members of the Deer, Buffalo and Gazelle Streets. This time Prince Donshu sent one of the leaders of his security guards, Tanjon, to handle the task of collecting and paying taxes to the Council of The Golden Path. Somewhere in the middle of collecting the tax money and paying it to the Council, Tanjon was ambushed. Tanjon offered his life to the Council for the failure of the delivery. He knew he could not return to the Wild Boar Tribe, for to fail is dishonorable, and he would be banned from the tribe.

The Council told Tanjon, "We will need you to help find out who is responsible for the robbery of the tax money." The Council also told Tanjon that it would be wise for him to remain in the town of Darnell as a guest of the Council until they decided their next move.

The Council felt they had to do something about the robbery, but what to do or who to send was a very serious decision. They first thought it would be wiser to send the Lion Tribe or the Jaguar Tribe to handle the matter of the ambush robbery and the death of the woman.

Then Dar-boo the Peace Keeper stood up and said, "All of the tribes of The Golden Path have suffered enough in the last two years, and the armies of each tribe should remain with their own. This year the men of each tribe are going on the traditional Warrior Army Quest which begins next week."

The Council said to Dar-boo, "Then who do we have at our Defense Department that we can call upon? We need someone who can handle the task of clearing out The Three Streets of The Golden Path, finding out who murdered that woman and who robbed the tax money."

Dar-boo said, "We have one more army you did not mention: the Women's Army of The Golden Path."

The Council said to Dar-boo, "We only voted on that two years ago. Do you really think they are ready for a mission of such magnitude?"

Dar-boo said, "Yes. But we can never know until we see how they perform in action."

The Council discussed it and agreed with Dar-boo. "This is their mission: the Women's Army will go to Deer Street, Buffalo Street, and Gazelle Street to investigate all these matters and make the area safe again. They will report to us when the matter is over. Go and tell the leader of the Women's Army she must have The Three Streets safe and clear before the Title Holder Games start."

Dar-boo said to the Council, "You must excuse me, for I have to go see Moo-su and let her know her army's mission."

Dar-boo travelled immediately to the Jaguar Tribe, to visit Lady Moo-su and tell her of the Council's approval for her army's first mission.

Moo-su told Dar-boo, "I am glad to undertake this mission. Queen Nstar of the Tiger Tribe and Keema of the Bear Tribe have become great leaders. All Title Holder women will be made officers. I will call for the peasants and the common blood to volunteer for the Women's Army. All women of The Golden Path are welcome in the first Women's Army."

Moo-su said, "I will ask for the women to meet me in the town of Darnell where we will devise our plan and the execution of it. It should take us two weeks for training of the troops. Then we will enter The Three Streets to claim order and submission by all means. Furthermore I will find whoever murdered the woman even if we have to shut down every business along The Three Streets."

Dar-boo said, "We must expect a revolt from the people of The Three Streets. Moreover, we expect the owners of the betting lounges are also seeking whoever is responsible for the murder of the woman, so that they won't have to endure being shut down. For the people who live or do business on The Three Streets the show must go on by any means necessary. The money must keep flowing at all times; little else matters."

The Three Streets are very tense for no one trusts anyone else. The Wild Boar Tribe is the most involved because their salary depends on the assessments of the tax monies, their cut in the betting lounges and their activities with the two gangs. Prince Donshu does not want any members of his tribe involved in any deviant acts or illegal activities. He has always wanted his tribe to abide by the laws, but there is always someone who wants to mess things up for the rest of the tribe.

There is a love triangle on The Three Streets and in order for the relationships to be successful there have to be some rules. The rules are:

- 49er Women will not gamble.
- Betting lounge owners will not get involved with someone else's business or women.
- Gang members will not mess with any betting lounge's business or women.

The Wild Boar Tribe while they are on The Three Streets, is to keep order and make sure everyone pays their taxes.

♏

As Dar-boo and Moo-su entered the town of Darnell, Moo-su quickly noticed the town was full of college students on spring break. There were people partying everywhere, including in the middle of the streets, without a care in life.

Dar-boo told Moo-su, "This town is home to the Council and the seven colleges. It will be a hard place for your army to settle, don't you think?"

Moo-su said, "A little playing after a lot of hard work won't hurt anyone. I think the ladies and I will do just great! You'll see Dar-boo."

Dar-boo said, "It will be a great task to bring different women from all over The Golden Path together and unite them as one. They must think as one, work as one, and attack as one. That will be a great sight to see, and if anyone can accomplish it, you can."

Moo-su said, "The first thing we will work on is respect for each other. Now how about you and I find a nice spot for us to have dinner and maybe party for a little while before tomorrow comes?"

Moo-su's journey to becoming head of the first Women's Army had not been an easy one. She sat at the dinner table and realized that she was enjoying watching the dancing. It was times like this that she really began to think about the husband she had lost over twenty years before in a war against the Cheetah Tribe. Comzar was a great leader and Moo-su missed him terribly.

♏

The next day arrived and Moo-su was the first to awake. Moo-su and Dar-boo met over breakfast and Moo-su asked Dar-boo, "Do you think any of the Title Holders will show up?"

Dar-boo answered, "But of course they will show up, for the women of The Golden Path are loyal and dedicated when it comes to defending their land. Trust me, they'll be here, Dar-boo said.

Dar-boo said to Moo-su, "We will meet with the women at the home of the Council. This home is available as long as necessary for the training of the Women's Army. We will be escorted to the compound by the Council service guards."

Dar-boo continued, "I know you will enjoy High Park Falls, the home of the Council. It has many waterfalls that lead to the Entertainment Castle, where the musical arts are performed."

When they arrived at High Park Falls, and Moo-su paused to enjoy the view. As she did so, she noticed a woman walking toward her. Moo-su said to Dar-boo, "Surely this woman walking toward us is not a volunteer for she is with child."

Dar-boo looked at Moo-su and said, "That woman is Teela, your first Title Holder to show up."

Moo-su looked in awe as the woman asked Dar-boo for some access codes. Dar-boo introduced the women, "Moo-su, this is Teela. Teela this is Moo-su, leader of the first Women's Army."

Teela said, "I am from the Lion Tribe, and it is an honor to meet you Lady Moo-su."

Moo-su replied, "I am from the Jaguar Tribe. I too am glad to meet you; however, you may now call me General Moo-su."

Dar-boo said to Moo-su, "Teela is Sebnala's twin sister and Nyrubi's cousin."

Moo-su asked Teela, "How will you be able to do this mission if you are with child?"

Teela said, "I wish to document the historical moments that the women of the army will encounter: how they come together, learn to respect each other's tribes and bond as one unit and one army. I will not be any burden to you, nor will I be in the way. Please understand, I need to do this. I have been guilty of wrongdoing. Now I would like to make things right, and this is a perfect opportunity for me to have time with the women of The Golden Path, let alone document it."

Moo-su looked at Dar-boo. Dar-boo said, "It is your decision to make."

Moo-su said to Teela, "I will allow you to be included in this army, but, any sign of problems or you hindering the mission and I will not hesitate to ask you to leave and return to your tribe."

Teela said, "Thank you General Moo-su. I will not let you down nor the women of The Golden Path no matter what tribe they are from." Teela also said, "I have studied every Title Holder from every tribe along The Golden Path, so when they arrive I can tell you who they are."

Dar-boo said, "That can be very useful. Thank you, Teela. The past is the past and you and your sister have put whatever happened to the two of you behind you, so lets start off fresh."

Just as Moo-su was finishing her conversation with Teela unexpected visitors arrived. Dar-boo and General Moo-su were surprised to see Prince Amtar of the Cheetah Tribe and Prince Donshu of the Wild Boar Tribe.

Dar-boo rushed over to greet them, "Is everything alright?"

Prince Amtar said, "Calm down. All is well. We have another matter we wish to speak to you about."

Prince Amtar said to Dar-boo, "I do not know what to do about my daughter Speed-Shay. She has forfeit her rights to perform in the Title Holders games to volunteer in the Women's Army. Moreover, now Prince Donshu's daughter Maysheara has joined the army as well."

Prince Donshu and Prince Amtar went on to tell Dar-boo how well both girls would do in the Title Holder Games if they participated. Then they tell Dar-boo that they have a plan that involves him. "We wish you would speak with both of our daughters and tell them it would not be a great idea for them to leave the Title Holder Games for the Women's Army."

Dar-boo along with Moo-su agreed they would not interfere with the two young ladies decision. Moo-su went on to say, "I think that what they are doing is very courageous. Your daughters are making decisions that will affect their lives forever. You should be very proud of both of these young ladies."

Dar-boo told the two Princes, "Your daughters will be in good hands." The two Princes agreed.

Dar-boo said to Prince Amtar, "It will be especially hard on you for you will have both your wife Graceshell and your daughter Speed-Shay in the Women's Army. But my friends you must go to lead your tribe in the Warriors Men's Quest for all tribes. You need to have your minds totally on that. Both of your families will be well taken care of so do not worry."

Prince Donshu of the Wild Boar Tribe and Prince Amtar thanked Dar-boo and Moo-su as they exited the room.

When the two Princes had left Moo-su said to Dar-boo, "We must have those two young ladies come before us so that we can talk with them."

Over the next three hours women came from all over The Golden Path to volunteer for the Women's Army. Teela said to Moo-su, "Over there is Keema and Brighthea of the Bear Tribe, and next to them is Samikia from the Salmon Tribe." Teela was excited when she saw the Title Holder from her own tribe. She shouted out, "There goes Nyrubi from the Lion and the Jaguar Tribes!" Moo-su was most happy to see Nyrubi among the women who were Title Holders. Teela continued, saying, "Nyrubi came here with my twin sister Sebnala." Teela was the first to notice that Sebnala had already broken the rules by bringing her royal cook, guards and servants. The army's official documents specifically said not to bring anything but what was needed for bed. Sebnala is the future Queen of the Lion Tribe since both Nyrubi and Shar-nu forfeited the throne, opting instead to marry. It appeared that Sebnala felt she was above the rules.

"Look over there, it is Queen Nstar," said Dar-boo.

"Isn't she the Queen of the Tiger Tribe?" Teela asked.

"Yes, you are right Teela." Dar-boo then looked at the document that listed all the names of the women Title Holders of all the tribes. He was quite pleased to see the turnout of all the Title Holder women, each having made the decision to put aside their differences and work together.

## TITLE HOLDERS ROLL CALL

- Queen Nstar, Tiger Tribe
- Moo-su, Jaguar Tribe
- Keema, Bear Tribe
- Nyrubi, Lion and Jaguar Tribe
- Handfurya, Hyena Tribe
- Sebnala, Lion Tribe
- Graceshell, Cheetah Tribe
- Brighthea, Bear Tribe
- Teela, Lion Tribe
- Samikia, Salmon Tribe
- Maysheara, Wild Boar Tribe
- Speed Shay, Cheetah Tribe

All of the Title Holder women who were expected had shown up except for one. The one Title Holder Woman who did not show was Shar-nu. She now lived outside of The Three Streets teaching children to read and write. She was married to Tryumph, who was one of the guards responsible for finding Nyrubi after she had been in the time vessel crash. Together they founded an orphanage that catered to the people who lived, worked and did business on The Three Streets. Shar -nu passed up her opportunity to become Queen of the Lion Tribe after King Zhaun. Shar-nu and her husband lived in an area called the Tree Patch, which is right outside of The Three Streets.

Moo-su told Dar-boo, "After everyone gets to know each other a bit I will call a meeting of all the volunteers. I would like to know why these women gave up their lives and their loved ones to volunteer for this army. I would also like to know what they had to sacrifice to be here today."

Moo-su went on to tell Dar-boo, "I will permit the Title Holders a night out on the town of Darnell tonight. This will be kind of like a ladies night out. It will give them time to get to know each other."

Dar-boo said to Moo-su, "As much as I would like to go with you, I will go and pay The Three Streets a little visit. I shall return first thing in the morning."

Moo-su said, "Be safe, because you know for every person you meet there will be two other people trying to play on you."

Dar-boo replied, "Yes I am familiar with The Three Streets and the customs that go along with them. I have been there many times, but this time I will go seeking a good friend of mine who just happens to be the best at gambling on The Three Streets. He is a regular from the Tiger Tribe but refused to compete in the Title Holder Games, so he was banned from his tribe. He has been there on The Three Streets ever since."

"Why wasn't he inducted into the Council Army?"

"Well, that's because one of the members of the Council is his father. He thinks he should be the King of the Tiger Tribe, not his half -sister Queen Nstar. However, instead of making problems for his tribe, he decided to leave before things escalated into something really disgraceful. His name is O'Hally and he is the son of Queen Cawann of the Tiger Tribe, also mother to Queen Nstar. I will go now Moo-su, even though I believe you will enjoy yourself much more than I will," said Dar-boo, as his loyal guards arrived to escort him to the door.

Moo-su sent for Teela and instructed her to inform all of the Title Holder women to assemble at once so she could speak with them. Upon approaching the women, Teela could see that they seemed to be having an argument.

Some of the Title Holder women were upset at Sebnala from the Lion Tribe for bringing her royal entourage with her. Being Title Holders themselves they too could have brought their royal cooks, servants, and guards. However, they obeyed the orders and had brought only what was absolutely necessary for them to sleep in.

Teela walked into the Title Holder Women's quarters to give them the message from Moo-su. Samikia from the Salmon Tribe, who is also sister to Sargent Carlay, asked Teela if she would go and talk to Sebnala because whenever anyone else tried to bring up the subject of her entourage it turned into an argument. She assured Teela that arguing was not intended nor needed at that point. Teela looked over at her twin sister and said to Samikia, "Yes, I will try talking to Sebnala."

Nyrubi walked over to Teela and gave her a hug. "I will go with you to talk to my little cousin Sebnala."

Teela and Nyrubi walk over to where Sebnala was resting. Teela said to her twin sister, "Hi Sebnala."

Sebnala turned around to see who was speaking to her. When she realized it was her twin sister Teela and her cousin Nyrubi she began jumping up and down with excitement. She immediately noticed Teela's extended belly and then she began rubbing the baby-filled stomach.

They all three hugged and then Nyrubi asked Sebnala, "Why did you bring all those servants when you were told not to?"

Sebnala replied, "I do not know. Maybe it has to do with the fact that I am the future Queen of the Lion Tribe. I need to look and feel my best at all times."

Teela said, "But the mission we are on calls for us to get down and dirty."

Sebnala looked surprised and asked, "Dirty?"

"Yes, dirty," replied Nyrubi.

Sebnala said to her two tribe members, "I guess you two are right. I will tell my guards that they will not be needed and to return home."

Just then Queen Nstar, who had been standing unnoticed behind them said, "We are too far from home to send them back now. Here is what we will do: your cook, servant, and guard will serve all of the Title Holder women. Moreover, they will be paid for their service." Then Queen Nstar from the Tiger Tribe told them all, "From this point on, you must all put aside where you are from, who you are and what you like and dislike about each other's tribes, so that you can become one unit—one body. You must get to a point of trusting and being there for each other. I have to believe that if I go into a battle that all you will have my back with your life, as I would give mine for yours."

⊠

As the Title Holders of the Women's Army of The Golden Path assembled in the conference room of the Council's home office in the town of Darnell, Moo-su asked Queen Nstar of the Tiger Tribe and Keema of the Bear Tribe to come and stand behind her so that she could introduce them and herself to the rest of the Title Holder women.

Moo-su introduced Queen Nstar and Keema then she said, "My name is Moo-su from the Jaguar Tribe. I have been assigned the rank of General in this New Women's Army of The Golden Path. Let me make myself absolutely clear, I am head of command, and the mission that was laid upon us will be accomplished by us. One day all of you women will have huge input into the way your tribes are ruled and now more than ever your leadership will be tested and absolutely essential for this task. The women who volunteered and left there loved ones behind deserve it and will demand great leadership from you all," said Moo-su as she locked eyes with the women. All eyes were on Moo-su as she continued speaking to the Title Holder women. They were in awe of General Moo-su, and she held their full attention. She said to the women, "I will spend the night with the women who volunteered for the army. You Title Holders will take one week to get to know each other, under Queen Nstar's charge, and your instructions are as follows."

The Women's eyes were huge. They could hardly contain themselves as they waited in anticipation to receive their first official orders.

She said, "Queen Nstar, you and the rest of the Title Holder women will go out and do the town. Now women we have a mission to complete. I will not let anything stand in our way of completing our objective. I caution you, for many of you this is your first time on your own, so to speak, and this is a completely different environment than you are used to. You are now The Women's Army of The Golden Path and that means that you are one unit, one family. When you are out tonight no one is to be alone. Be your sister's keeper, carry yourself with pride and dignity and use diplomacy and wisdom in all matters.

"Know that there are people against our army and they would like nothing more than to see us fail. Unfortunately some of those closest to us are the very ones who are hoping for or predicting our failure. This includes some of our own husbands, tribe members, a number of old men and surprisingly some old women who think a woman's place is to be in the house making babies and serving their family day and night. How we handle ourselves now will determine whether or not women are going to be respected and highly regarded as soldiers. For there to be a Women's Army in the future it is imperative that we complete the objective of this mission with strength and conviction.

"All of you are Title Holders, and I expect leadership and respect from each one of you. You are the best of the best. I know it is hard when you put together all these great women and hope that everything will work out. You all had to go through a lot to be Title Holder women, so put aside all of your differences and become as one. For that is what it is going to take for this mission to be a success and for each of you to reach your full potential.

"One more thing," Moo-su said. "Cherish this night out for tomorrow we begin our training."

Moo-su dismissed the Title Holder women, and that is when Teela asked if she could accompany her when she had dinner with the volunteer troops that night. Moo-su said, "But of course you can." Moo-su told Teela, "I thought I would have to visit the volunteers all by myself, and for that I thank you Teela."

As the women cleared the room Moo-su asked Teela, "Do you know which two are Speed-Shay and Maysheara?"

Teela looked around and then said, "There they are, over there. They are speaking with Speed-Shay's mother, Graceshell of the Cheetah Tribe." Moo-su was amazed at what she saw. A mother and daughter in the same army.

Moo-su walked over to greet Graceshell, Speed-Shay and Maysheara. Moo-su told Graceshell how very pleased she was to have Graceshell among them, and how very proud she must be of her daughter Speed-Shay and her friend Maysheara. Moo-su looked at Speed-Shay and Maysheara and said to them, "I have heard great things about the two of you. "

Maysheara asked, "How can that be?"

Moo-su replied, "Your fathers stopped to have a word with me about you two while on their way to the Council for the hearing to let your people, Maysheara, the Wild Boar Tribe, receive their own land along The Golden Path. They told me how you both forfeited your rights to be in the Title Holder Games in order to enlist in the Women's Army. Tell me how you came to your decision."

Speed-Shay told Moo-su, "I wanted to experience and see all of The Golden Path for myself instead of hearing about it from others. I also want to see all of these great women in their own right come together as one. Furthermore I wanted to be here with my mother, Graceshell, to see it all."

"Maysheara, what about you?" Moo-su asked.

"Well I did not want my good friend Speed-Shay to be alone, because when my tribe moved outside of The Three Streets and I was new in that area Speed-Shay was my friend even if we were from a different tribe, and I thank her for that."

Speed-Shay said, "Thank you, Maysheara. You have helped me too."

Moo-su told the two young ladies, "You can come with Teela and me to visit the volunteer troops tonight, or you may go with the rest of the Title Holder women to have a ladies night out."

They both asked Moo-su if she would be upset if they went with the other Title Holder women. Moo-su said, "No! Go and enjoy yourselves, for tomorrow will be a big day for us all." The two girls departed.

Nyrubi walked up to Moo-su and asked her how she was doing and if there was anything she could do for her. Moo-su said, "Yes, as a matter of fact, you can look out for the two young ones, Speed- Shay and Maysheara. I know that Speed-Shay's mother is here, but we don't want Graceshell to be accused of giving unfair attention to them." Then Moo-su hugged Nyrubi and said, "Thank you."

⊠

That night, as the Title Holder women of The Golden Path began exploring the nightlife of the town of Darnell, they learned that the parties were largely college kids celebrating before the big quick ball game to be played the next day. It would be the High Park Wavine against the Keromp Beach Rams and the biggest game of the year. The town of Darnell would be filled with Wild kids partying all night.

Sebnala told the other Title Holders, "There is no way we can have fun in the town with babies running all over. Tonight the town of Darnell is not the one for us. We could go to The Three Streets to have some fun."

Brighthea said, "Queen Nstar said we are to conduct an investigation on The Three Streets and you all want to visit there? I am not sure that that is a good idea right now."

Maysheara said to the others, "It's not very far away. We could be back before anyone noticed we were gone."

Handfuria of the Hyena Tribe said, "If we go to The Three Streets we must look out for any trick to make us turn against each other. We must remember who is in charge and why we are there. Listen and keep a good eye on your surroundings, for on The Three Streets anything goes beside death, so we must stick together."

Brighthea and Graceshell told the rest of the women, they did do not think it would be wise to go The Three Streets without the rest of the army. "However," they agreed, "the decision is Queen Nstar's to make."

Queen Nstar looked at Keema and gave the OK for the Title Holder women to go and have some fun on The Three Streets instead of staying in the town of Darnell.

⊠

Dar-boo was in The Three Streets that night to visit his good friend O'Hally from the Tiger Tribe. They were seated at one of the tables in the betting lounges on Gazelle Street. Dar-boo had decided not tell anyone, O'Hally included, about the Women's Army and their mission.

The Title Holder women entered The Three Streets of The Golden Path and found themselves near the same betting lounge, although they did not know Dar-boo was inside.

Keema asked, "Who will stay with the women who are under age?"

Nyrubi said, "I will stay with Maysheara, Samikia, Speed-Shay, and Handfuria."

Graceshell said, "No, Speed-Shay is my daughter. I shall stay.

Then Brighthea said, "It's OK I will stay. Go and enjoy yourselves."

Queen Nstar asked Brighthea, "Are you sure?"

"I'm very sure," said Brighthea.

The Title Holder women entered the betting lounge and Dar-boo was the first to notice them.

Dar-boo told O'Hally, "I must get some air."

The two men exited the betting lounge without the Title Holders seeing them, which was good for Dar-boo because he did not want O'Hally to see Queen Nstar. his half-sister, for it could hamper the investigation.

While the other Title Holder women were enjoying themselves in the betting lounges Samikia, Speed-Shay, Maysheara and Handfuria decided to go to the market for a little shopping. Before they entered the market Brighthea covered her face with her hood so that no one would look directly at her.

Samikia was looking at something she liked when Brighthea walked up to her. As the two women were talking, Brighthea pushed back her hood to get a better look at the item. A woman and her boyfriend walked into the market and within seven seconds the man could not keep his eyes off Brighthea. Speed-Shay said to Brighthea, "That man will not stop looking at you." Brighthea covered her head with her hood, but it was too late. The woman asked Brighthea, "Why are you looking at my man?"

Brighthea told the woman, "I did not say anything to your boyfriend, yet I do apologize for any misunderstanding."

The woman told Brighthea, "There is no misunderstanding. I saw you trying to talk to my man. You should ask around and see what happened to the last woman who tried to talk to my man."

Samikia said to Brighthea, "I think we should be going now."

Speed-Shay, Handfuria, Maysheara, and Brighthea walked outside of the market only to find themselves surrounded by women they had never seen before. They were members of the all-female gang who called themselves the 49er Women.

As they are in the middle of Gazelle Street, face-to-face with these women it seemed that there was no way out for the Title Holder women except to fight. "The 49er Women seem very upset, or maybe that is just the way they are," Brighthea thought to herself.

Brighthea addressed the 49er Women, "I will only say this one more time: I did not try to hit on her man. If you do not believe me, there is nothing else to be said. Then let it be." Brighthea then told Speed-Shay, Maysheara, Handfurya and Samikia to go, because she did not want them to be injured in a fight. They refused to leave, telling her that they would not leave without her.

There were nine 49er Women present and five Title Holder women. Nevertheless the fight started. The 49er Women are fearless when in a fight, and the Title Holder women were right in the thick of things.

⊠

Dar-boo and O'Hally saw a crowd jumping and screaming at the fight scene. O'Hally raced over to stop the fight as Dar-boo faded into the crowd, for he did not want the Title Holder women to see him. O'Hally stopped the fight, walked over to the 49er Women and said to them, "You know the rules: no one fights on The Three Streets unless all bets have been made. Ladies, please allow me just a moment to collect all bets, and then you may resume your battle."

O'Hally yelled, "What will it be? We all know who the 49er Women are; however these other women, these unknowns, these intruders, these gatecrashers have the audacity to come here and challenge our champions. I don't know who they think they are, but I will tell you this, for some reason I think the 49er Women have a real fight on their hands for the first time. I am betting on the outsider women, so place your bet."

Everyone started yelling and placing bets. O'Hally walked over to where Dar-boo was standing and said, "The 49er Women have never lost a fight. I have gotten rich off them because when they fight they fight to the death, but you know, I just cannot get it out of my mind how tenacious those women were when I walked over there. They were going toe-to-toe with the 49er Women."

O'Hally returned and stood in the middle of the circle. The crowd was excited and ready for the fight to resume. They were finally going to see a new opponent fight the 49er Women instead of the same old card of the 49er Women vs. the Dark Rangers or the Village Daggers.

Dar-boo watched as the Title Holder women readied themselves. He was thoroughly impressed with what he saw.

O'Hally announced, "Ladies and gentlemen, we are ready to rumble!"

Brighthea looked at Samikia, Speed-Shay, Handfurya, and Maysheara and then said to O'Hally, "We are ready."

At that moment, she felt invincible. She was confident in knowing that her Title Holder sisters had her back. She felt that she and the other women could take on the world as long as they stuck together. Then the fight started.

Back at the betting lounge, the rest of the Title Holder women were enjoying themselves. Nyrubi looked outside and before she could relay to the others what she saw, a man yelled out, "Fight, fight! There's a fight outside."

Nyrubi and the other Title Holder women rushed out to where the two groups were fighting. Graceshell realized it was Speed-Shay and the other Title Holder women who were in the fight. Graceshell saw her daughter and instinctively she moved to defend her child. Sebnala caught her by the arm and said, "Wait."

Queen Nstar walked up to where the women were fighting and stopped it. Then she asked the group who they were. They refused to answer her. Queen Nstar went on to tell the crowd, "This little fight is now over. If it continues, I guarantee, no one here will like the outcome and that includes bystanders. Please look around you. You will notice that you are surrounded by women who on my command will attack. So what is your pleasure?"

The entire crowd looked around and saw that Queen Nstar was right. The 49er Women's creed was still to fight to the death.

Queen Nstar said, "We will calmly walk away, however, if you give us no choice I will have you all finished."

Queen Nstar told all of the Title Holder women to get themselves ready to attack. Graceshell got herself in position to take out the leader of the 49er Women.

Just as the two female groups were about to engage in a battle O'Hally thought he recognized someone. He said to Dar-boo, "Dar-boo, is that who I think it is? Oh no it is. That is my sister, Queen Nstar. What is she doing here?"

O'Hally rushed over to stop the fight before it started. He yelled, "All bets are off!"

The crowd rebelled and shouted wildly to O'Hally, "Who do you think you are?" The leader of the Village Daggers said to O'Hally, "You cannot keep making up rules as you go. Who gave you the authority to be in charge anyway?"

O'Hally turned on the man and bellowed out, "Until any one of you can beat me in anything, I am now and will continue to be the rule maker. Right now I said all bets are off. Now go enjoy yourselves for there will not be any fight here tonight."

O'Hally looked for Dar-boo, but he was nowhere to be found. Nyrubi went to thank the man whoever he was, but Queen Nstar said to Nyrubi, "There is no need to thank him."

O'Hally said, "Is that any way to treat your own brother?"

The rest of the Title Holder women looked on in awe.

"You are not my brother. You left us remember?" Then Queen Nstar said to the other Women's group, who she now knew were called the 49er Women, "You have not seen the last of us. It will not be words that pass between us on our next encounter."

Queen Nstar told the Title Holder women to back out slowly as they left The Three Streets. Queen Nstar asked Brighthea, Speed-Shay, Maysheara, Samikia and Handfurya if they were all right, as they looked at each other. Then they started jumping and laughing with each other. "We did it. We stuck together, and we had each other's backs."

Queen Nstar said, "You did. The five of you did extremely well, and I am proud of you all. I must say to you though, I am very sorry for leaving the five of you alone. I assure you that that will never ever happen again."

⊠

Dar-boo arrived in the town of Darnell to let Moo-su know where the Title Holder women had gone and what took place on The Three Streets. He told her that the young group of Handfurya, Speed-Shay, Samikia, Maysheara and Brighthea had engaged themselves in a fighting attraction.

"The Title Holder women do not know that I witnessed the entire incident between the two female fighting groups."

"Who were the other group of women?" asked Moo-su.

Dar-boo replied, "I had never laid eyes on them, but my good friend O'Hally knew of them and informed me that they are vicious fighters. He also told me that he'd been getting rich off of them for years by betting on them whenever they fight. They call themselves the 49er Women, and their home is somewhere inside of Money Rock Mountain, which is outside The Three Streets."

Moo-su said, "I take it you do not want the Title Holders to know you were there, so we can see if they tell us what happened on their own?"

"Yes, that is exactly what I am thinking."

That night when the Title Holder women returned to the town of Darnell, Queen Nstar told Moo-su and Dar-boo what had happened at The Three Streets. Queen Nstar took full responsibility for what had happened and promised it would never happen again under her command.

"I expected you would apologize, and I do accept the apology," said Moo-su. "By way of discipline, the next two weeks while we are here, training, the Title Holder women will carry out the duty of serving all meals."

"Yes, I understand," said Queen Nstar to the General.

Dar-boo then asked Queen Nstar how she felt about seeing her brother, O'Hally. Queen Nstar replied, "We did not need his help in any way, and I will leave it at that."

Moo-su told Queen Nstar to have Brighthea, Samikia, Handfurya, Maysheara and Speed-Shay report to her at once.

Moo-su asked the five Title Holder women, "How did it feel to be in real battle, and to have each other's backs?"

Maysheara told Moo-su how great a leader Brighthea had been in instructing them how to prepare. "She thought about us before herself. Thank you for that, Lady Brighthea." The others agreed.

That night everyone at the Title Holder quarters was asleep except for Nyrubi, Samikia, Maysheara and Keema. Nyrubi asked Keema to tell her all about who Hardstone was and how he was killed, as well as the Battle of Cottonburg. Keema told them about Hardstone, avoiding details of his death. "I will however tell you all about the water caves." Keema told the ladies how the walls of the water cave tell the history of The Golden Path, as they all fell asleep.

The next day the Council and all tribe leaders met at the Hyena Tribe territory to vote on the Wild Boar Tribe's petition to become part of The Golden Path, with full membership and responsibilities and territory on The Golden Path.

Chancellor Shenot of the Hyena Tribe welcomed King Zhaun and the other leaders, acknowledging they were anxious to finish this matter so they could get back to their army and resume the Male Quest.

86

"You know why we are here, so let's get the voting started."

Just as they were about to vote, they were interrupted by loud noises coming from outside the Chancellor quarters. All of the men rushed to investigate.

When they finally got to where the noise was coming from, they were in for a surprise, for it was Princess Meaira from the Gorilla Tribe. Prince Amtar said abruptly to Princess Meaira, "What do you have to say for yourself before you are put to death?"

Princess Meaira asked if she could go in front of the Council to petition them for acceptance into the Title Holder Games.

The leaders said, "There is no way that you will be allowed to participate in any Golden Path activity."

Princess Meaira requested the matter be put to a vote.

The Council told Princess Meaira they could not vote on the matter because two of the Council members, Queen Nstar and Dar-boo, were away.

"Furthermore, you know that Queen Nstar cannot stand the sight of you," Leo-Paul of the Lion Tribe said to Princess Meaira. "I suggest you leave before we start to remember all of the atrocities that you and the Gorilla Tribe have committed against The Golden Path and its people."

Princess Meaira said, "My people were wrong for letting the Invaders influence us in attacking the tribes of The Golden Path. But if you do not let me compete in the Title Holder Games I cannot be responsible for the actions that my tribe may again take because of your unfairness toward us." Princess Meaira smiled arrogantly at the leaders of The Golden Path and the Council. "The great Peace Keeper Comboos made the rules specifically to keep wars away from tribe and keep the tribes aware of each other. And that rule calls for participation in the Title Holder Games."

The Council replied to Princess Meaira, "Even if for some strange reason we agreed to allow you to compete in the Title Holder Games, we still have members of the Council and leadership who are not present. Therefore, we simply cannot vote on that matter at this time."

Princess Meaira asked, "Who is not present?"

Afro-Light of the Jaguar Tribe answered, "Queen Nstar of the Tiger Tribe and the Peace Keeper Dar-boo are not present."

Princess Meaira shouted, "Queen Nstar? What does she have to do with this matter? Queen Nstar is the reason my father was killed, and I refuse to let her be the deciding vote on whether my tribe can compete in the Games."

Princess Meaira walked over to where King Zhaun was standing and said, "I am the new leader of the Gorilla Tribe, and I will try to keep my tribe from attacking The Golden Path. Do not make me do otherwise for their shall be more bloodshed."

The Council said to Princess Meaira, "We will not vote on this matter until the next time we meet."

Princess Meaira asked, "And when might that be?"

The Council said, "In three months, after the Title Games are over."

Princess Meaira said to every leader of The Golden Path and the leaders of the Council, "Well then there will be no need for us to meet again." She was furious at having to wait for the next meeting to take place, a meeting that would come too late for her to participate in the upcoming Title Holder Games.

Princess Meaira felt that she should have the right to be in the Title Holder Games and the decision should not be left up to Queen Nstar, her utmost enemy.

Leo-Paul of the Lion Tribe said to the Council, "Are we just going to let her walk in her, make demands on us and threaten our lives if we do not concede? We should have her beheaded or at the very least lock her up. Do not forget the countless gruesome murders that her tribe and the Elephant tribe have inflicted upon the tribes of The Golden Path. I say let's kill her now while we have the chance."

King Zhaun said to Princess Meaira, "If you think for one moment we will be intimidated by your threats, you are vastly mistaken. You will see how the tribes of The Golden Path handle such bullying. I think that it is wise that you leave this room right now, for I cannot tell you what will happen if you stay one moment longer. I feel the leaders of The Golden Path will have their armies ready to attack you before you can attack us, so you go and prepare your tribe. What happened two years ago must be finished."

Then King Zhaun told the leaders of The Golden Path, "Go and alarm your armies. It is apparent that we still have much unfinished business with the Gorilla and the Elephant Tribes."

Chief Grawn of the Bear Tribe told the Council and the leaders of the Golden Tribe, "This must be the final battle. There must be no possibility of war with these tribes ever again. I think it will be wise to rule, when the war with the Elephant and Gorilla tribes is over, that they may not have an army. We cannot keep going to war with these tribes every two years. We must put a stop to it once and for all."

The Council told the leaders of The Golden Path, "All of you and your armies should go east, while all of the villages and towns will defend the west side. We the Council will wait for the Women's Army to return from their first mission. Then we will also join you in this final attack against the Elephant and Gorilla Tribe."

Emperor Albertine said, "This time we go to war with them it will be different. We were on the defensive being attacked on our own land the last time. This time we will do the attacking on their land."

The Council asked, "Do you think we will have to go outside The Golden Path?"

"Yes we will, because I have it on good authority that the Elephant and Gorilla tribes have moved further east in the Old Land, near the Real Sea."

Afro-Light asked the other leader, "If we are to go east to launch a surprise attack against these tribes who will secure The Golden Path?"

Prince Amtar answered. "We can ask the people of the towns and villages to stand guard on the west side of The Golden Path, while all of the tribes of The Golden Path will go east to the Old Land to attack the Elephant and Gorilla tribes on their own land."

⊠

As Princess Meaira was on the way back to the Old Land her husband Landlock told her how she could defeat the members of The Golden Path. He said, "Last time we went to war with the tribes of The Golden Path we were under someone else's command. The Game Hunters were in charge. This time we will be in charge of the Game Hunters, all four who remain alive."

"How is that?" Princess Meaira asked.

"After the last war was over the Elephant Tribe and their leader, Matriarch Elitcal, captured the four remaining Game Hunters and made them her personal slaves. So along with the Elephant Tribe and the Game Hunters, with a plan we will finally be able to defeat the tribes of The Golden Path."

"When will we be able to look at these so-called plans?" Princess Meaira asked.

Landlock said, "Well we could send a message ahead to the Elephant Tribe asking to speak with them on the matter of the war against The Golden Path."

⌧

Both Princess Meaira and her husband entered the Elephant Tribe Territory and were welcomed there, as always.

Queen Elitcal asked Princess Meaira if she and her husband would stay for dinner. Princess Meaira graciously accepted the offer.

Princess Meaira spoke to Queen Elitcal about the humongous loss of men each of their tribes had suffered at the hands of the tribes of The Golden Path. "Furthermore, the way they did our men in the village of Michelgray was unacceptable and a disgrace to our ancestors and our tribes."

Princess Meaira went on to tell Queen Elitcal, "The last time we engaged in a war with the tribes of The Golden Path we were under the command of others—the Game Hunters and Hardstone. This time when we attack … "

Queen Elitcal quickly interrupted Princess Meaira. "When we attack? I do not think so. This time it is going to go my way. Here is the plan: the people of my tribe have been working hard to become industrialized like the Lion Tribe of The Golden Path. I will not take my people into another war with The Golden Path or anyone for that matter without reason, for the loss of life is so great … "

Princess Meaira said to Queen Elitcal, "In the last war against The Golden Path we did not expect victory we did not plan well. The key to success is in the plan itself. I have a plan to attack The Golden Path while they will be enjoying the Title Holder Games."

Queen Elitcal did not approve of the plan that Princess Meaira described. Then Queen Elitcal told Princess Meaira she had a plan of her own, one which took a lot of hard work to plan and prepare to execute. "We will talk more after we enjoy some dinner."

After dinner Queen Elitcal asked Princess Meaira if she knew the real reason that her tribe voted to move east near the Real Sea. She walked Princess Meaira to a spot in her palace where it overlooked the Real Sea Mountains and also The Real Sea.

The Real Sea is a sea that is between the Real World and the Land of the Seven.

Queen Elitcal told Princess Meaira to look out at the sea and tell her what she saw.

Princess Meaira looked and saw something she had never seen before in her life. She quickly asked, "What are those things standing in the water?"

Queen Elitcal explained, "What you are looking at are what the people in the Real World call 'boats.' The big ones that you see in the Real Sea are called 'ships.' My tribe, along with the Game Hunters, has been busy making the ships. My plan is to capture the men from every tribe of The Golden Path and place them all on the ship that we have specifically made for them. The Game Hunters will take the men and sell them all to the Real World as slaves. Then and only then will I allow the Game Hunters to return to mate with the women of The Golden Path.

"This plan calls for you, Princess Meaira, to take your tribe's army and invade the town of Darnell. Kill just enough people to get the tribes of The Golden Path to take notice and come to the aid of the town. When they come to the town the people will tell them we went east to the Old Land. They will pursue us into the Real Sea Mountains, and when they do that they will walk right into our trap. They will never even know it when they board the ship. It will be camouflaged to blend in with the Real Sea Mountains, and they will believe they are still on solid ground. In reality they will be on the ship that will sail them away to the Real World. Then we will be able to take over The Golden Path."

Queen Elitcal also told Princess Meaira she must make sure that the tribes of The Golden Path pursue. "They must follow you into the Real Sea Mountains for our plan to succeed. I cannot emphasize how important it is for their army to follow you into the mountains, because my people cannot afford another defeat to the armies of The Golden Path." Then she said, "Take your tribe, Princess Meaira, and start the first phase of the plan at once."

As Moo-su led the Title Holder women towards The Three Streets she told Queen Nstar about the attack on the town of Darnell that had occurred while the town was enjoying the open ceremony for the Title Holder Games. Moo-su had been given a message from the Council, notifying her of the attack but telling her that her assistance would not be required to defend Darnell. Moo-su was to continue her focus on cleaning up The Three Streets and investigating the woman's murder. It also said:

*"The Men's army of all tribes will handle the matter once and for all. We will go east to finish off what the Elephant and the Gorilla tribes have started.*

Moo-su said to Queen Nstar, "I do not know why, but I have a strange feeling that something unexpected is about to happen. I would be much more at ease about the attack in the town of Darnell if the Council would let us help in the counterattack against the Elephant and Gorilla tribes."

Queen Nstar said, "Maybe the investigation will be a quick one. Then we would be able to return to the town of Darnell faster than anticipated and be of some assistance to the men of The Golden Path."

Queen Nstar also told Moo-su, "Brighthea informed me that before the confrontation between our women and the 49er Women, the woman who started the fight made reference to an incident with another woman. She said that the last woman who happened to look at her man was no longer here."

"Well then we should start with the 49er Women first," Moo-su said. "We will go to The Three Streets to ask some questions, and if we do not get the right answers we will threaten to close down all businesses including the betting lounges until the investigation is complete."

Moo-su led the Women's Army of The Golden Path into The Three Streets to began their murder investigation. It had now been two months since the dead woman had been found behind the betting lounges. The army combed the town asking about the woman, and all of their tips led to the 49er woman who had started the fight.

As the Women's Army entered Deer Street they meet up with Dar-boo. Dar-boo is from Deer Street, and he also had been doing his own investigation on who murdered the woman. Dar-boo told Moo-su that the only people left to question were the 49er Women. "To get to them," he said, "you have to go to Money Rock Mountain, which is right outside The Three Streets."

⊠

As the Women's Army approached Money Rock Mountain they came under attack. Moo-su told Queen Nstar to take the right side of the mountain and had Keema take some of the troops to the left side of the mountain. "We will meet at the front entrance," she said.

The fighting went on for several hours and the Women's Army was advancing inward. That was exactly what the 49er Women did not want, because they did not want anyone to know the gold they sold to the tribes and The Three Streets was actually from within Money Rock Mountain. They are prepared to defend it with their lives.

The fighting became fierce as the Women's Army got closer to the entrance of the mountain. Both sides took a lot of losses in the battle after one day of fighting.

The leader of the 49er Women sent a message to the leader of the Women's Army. Moo-su received the message, which stated that the leader of The 49er Women wished to speak with the leader of the Women's Army at a location outside of Money Rock Mountain. This was an attempt to divert the Women's Army away from the mountain and the gold, however, Queen Nstar had already found some gold and brought it to Moo-su.

Moo-su said to Queen Nstar, "This is undoubtedly the real reason behind the unexpected attack." Moo-su went on to say, "The women would have attacked anyone who came close to Money Rock Mountain in order to guard their secret about the gold in the mountain."

"I will meet with the leader of the 49er Women. I must let her know that we are only here to do our job, and that is to find out who murdered the woman behind the betting lounges two months ago. Furthermore, we couldn't care less about their gold or who they sold it to, and we will keep their secret. We will see this mission through down to the last woman standing if need be. We are willing and ready for a long battle."

Moo-su along with Queen Nstar and Nyrubi went to the entrance of the mountain to meet with Tozara, the leader of the 49er Women.

Tozara told Moo-su, "I want you off this mountain right this instant. I will only tell you and your army this once. After that, if you refuse to leave then you give me no choice but to attack you and your army to the end if we have to."

Moo-su walked up to Tozara and told her, "We are not afraid of any of your threats. I assure you, my army is able to finish all of you off. You must cooperate with us in our investigation of who killed the woman behind the betting lounges two months ago. We also know that there is gold in these mountains, but that is not our concern. We wish only to complete our mission, which is to find the murderer and return with her or him so they can face justice. This is our only objective. No one wants the business on The Three Streets to be shut down until the investigation is completed, and that can be avoided if we can complete our mission now and be on our way." Moo-su told Tozara, "We have been asking around about the murder and all tips lead to a certain 49er Woman. I was told that one of your women admitted that she accused a woman of stealing her man and so she took care of her. If that is true, then all you have to do is turn her over to us. Let her go in front of the Council and tell them what happened and why it happened. I am sure the Council will come to the conclusion that she is not guilty of any wrongdoing since their is no stealing and no killing allowed on The Three Streets, and they will set her free," said Moo-su.

Tozara told Moo-su, "I know exactly who you are looking for; however, she is dead. She was one of our first casualties last night in the fighting between our two factions. Her body lies right over there. It has yet to be retrieved for burial."

Moo-su said, "If what you tell me and show me is true then I see no need to continue this investigation any longer. We will return with our mission complete. Furthermore your secret will always be safe with us."

Tozara told Moo-su, "I must say it is a great thing to see a real army of women. It's about time women were recognized for their amazing abilities to negotiate and fight for what they believe is right. I am just so sorry that we had to meet under these circumstances. I would have liked the opportunity to have met and become friends instead of meeting in battle."

Moo-su said to Tozara, "I agree. I would like very much to come back sometime and visit you if you would allow me."

Tozara looked at the woman and said, "You and your army will always be welcomed here at Money Rock Mountain."

Samikia asked Speed-Shay and Handfurya, "What do you think the two leaders are talking about? Do you think the 49er Women will try to do something to our leaders?"

Maysheara answered, "It is a 'rule of war' that when the warring leaders agree to meet with each other all fighting is on hold. This is to assure that the safety of both leaders is not compromised. If by chance someone does break the rule, they will be found by the Council's Army and put to death."

Graceshell said to all of the Title Holder women, "Whatever they are saying they should make it quick; a fierce storm is heading this way. If we are to return to the town of Darnell in time to assist the Men's Army of The Golden Path we need to leave immediately."

⊠

The gathering of the Men's Army was a sight to see. All of the tribes and their great leaders were coming together for one cause: to finish off the Elephant and Gorilla Tribes once and for all.

The tribe leaders ultimately had agreed that coming together as one power would be most effective, but like every group they needed one person to be in charge. They decided that the oldest and most experienced tribal leader amongst them would take charge of the mission. That wise and deserving leader was King Zhaun of the Lion Tribe.

King Zhaun asked Afro-Light and Emperor Albertine the possible ways to get to the Real Sea Mountains. Afro-Light told King Zhaun, "There are but two ways: we can go around it, which will take at least three days, or we can go through it."

"If only Dar-boo was with us," King Zhaun thought to himself. He then told Afro-Light, Leo-Paul and Chief Grawn to take their armies and go to the right tunnel of the Real Sea Mountains. Emperor Albertine, Prince Amtar and Chancellor Shenot would take the left tunnel. "And I," he said, "along with my Royal Army will take the middle tunnel."

General Tex and Sergeant Carlay of the Salmon Tribe asked Emperor Albertine if it would be all right if they were to go with King Zhaun through the middle tunnel, and the Emperor gave his OK.

Leo-Paul said to all of the leaders, "Everything has been going great up to this point, a little too great if you ask me. I have a strange feeling that an ambush is iminent."

Prince Amtar said, "These tunnels should meet up somewhere in the mountains, and all three tunnels must be checked to see if any of the Elephant or Gorilla Tribes are waiting in them for a surprise attack."

King Zhaun told all of the leaders of The Golden Path, "No man knows what is about to happen to him. Whatever happens, we each must continue to move forward in growth and life. Always remember that the Higher Power is with us. Leaders of The Golden Path Tribes, lead your armies into the Real Sea Mountains to search for the Elephant and Gorilla tribes' armies."

⊠

As the armies of The Golden Path tribes entered the Real Sea Mountains, Queen Elitcal was waiting patiently for them to fall right into her trap. She and Princess Meaira sat at her perch overlooking the Real Seal Mountains and the Real Sea. At first Princes Meaira could not see where The Golden Path Tribe armies were, then Queen Elitcal pointed them out. Next Queen Elitcal told Princess Meaira, "Go and tell the army and the Game Hunters."

They were very careful not to reveal themselves until the armies of The Golden Path were on the ships. Queen Elitcal was going over the plan in her head, satisfied that it was on track. "They will be thinking they are somewhere inside the Real Sea Mountains, yet just as they begin to move we will drop the trap and quickly move the ship into the sea. The faster we get them out to sea the better our chances of nothing going wrong."

When The Golden Path armies met in the middle of the Real Sea Mountains they were anticipating finding the Gorilla and the Elephant tribes so they could launch a surprise attack against them.

As the armies lit their torches they began asking each other, "Where are the Gorilla and Elephant tribes?" and "What part of the mountain are we in?"

King Zhaun sent two troops ahead to scout the area, looking specifically for the two tribes. He cautioned them to make sure they were not seen. "We will wait for seven minutes then follow."

Just as the scouts moved out of their sight the trap was sprung. Nets fell from the ceiling on top of the tribes. The plan had gone splendidly for Queen Elitcal.

The next step was for the Game Hunters to take all of the men and sell them to the Real World as slaves.

Queen Elitcal received the great news that her plan was a complete success. She then asked Princess Meaira if she actually knew what all of this meant. She said to her friend, "This means no more men in The Golden Path. No men to rule over us. No men to be in the tribes' armies to attack us and no men armies to stop us from taking over The Golden Path. We will be rid of the men once and for all."

Queen Elitcal continued, "After the two Game Hunters return from the Real World to give us the signal that the men of The Golden Path have been sold into slavery, we will attack the rest of The Golden Path.

"For now we will celebrate this occasion, for we have done the unthinkable. We have captured all of the men of The Golden Path armies. Both of us should be proud of our tribes, and the way we used the Game Hunters to our advantage. Tomorrow the prisoners will demand to speak with us, but we will not say a word to them.

"Princess Meaira, I know you would like to do away with Queen Nstar, but first we must do away with Dar-boo."

Princess Meaira asked, "Who is Dar-boo?"

"He is someone so powerful and spiritual that as long as he is still alive the tribes of The Golden Path have a chance of defeating us," replied Queen Elitcal. "With him alive the tribes of The Golden Path will not stop until they have avenged themselves. We must find Dar-boo first thing tomorrow. We must know for sure whether or not he was captured with the others."

Queen Elitcal is a great Plan Master, but she knows that the Peace Keeper Dar-boo is the supreme Plan Master of the entire Land of Seven. In order to be the best Plan Master she must eliminate the Peace Keeper Dar-boo.

Led by Moo-su of the Jaguar Tribe, the very first mission of the Women's Army of The Golden Path was completed. They were on their way back to the town of Darnell when the storm that Graceshell had warned of was upon them. The storm became so bad that they could go no further.

After the army found cover, Queen Nstar asked Dar-boo and Moo-su if she should tell the army to stay in cover until sunrise. Both Dar-boo and Moo-su agreed that they should bunk down for the night.

Nyrubi, Brighthea, Sebnala and the rest were enjoying dinner when they noticed something very wrong. It was Teela. She looked as though she was ready to have her baby right there and then. All of the Title Holder Officers gathered around Teela to see what needed to be done. Nyrubi asked everyone to be calm and then asked if anyone knew how to deliver a baby. "Dar-boo do you?"

He replied, "I have done many things, but deliver a baby? No, not me."

Keema stepped up and said shyly, "I have some experience in birthing babies."

Moo-su said, "If Keema will deliver the baby all of us will assist."

Brighthea placed herself behind Keema and told her, "You can do this. It is your calling to bring this baby into The Golden Path's world, and I thank you for that Keema."

Sebnala walked over to where Teela, her twin sister was on the verge of giving birth. Sebnala lifted Teela's head up and placed it on her lap. It was a wonderful night as all these great women who had come together to fight were bringing a new life into the world. The storm was at its strongest when Teela gave birth to a baby girl. Then she handed the baby girl to Speed-Shay, Samikia, Handfurya and Maysheara, so they could bathe her.

Dar-boo asked Teela, "What is the baby girl's name?"

Teela looked at all of the Title Holder women and said, "I wish for all of you to be her Godmothers, should anything happen to me. And I wish for Nyrubi to name my baby girl."

That night they had a ceremony to bless and dedicate the baby to the Supreme Being. Nyrubi named the baby girl Olamae.

While everyone was celebrating the birth of Olamae, Dar-boo was talking to Sebnala and Queen Nstar about how proud he was of the new Women's Army, yet he felt there was still something missing.

"I cannot put my finger on exactly what it is, but I will figure it out soon."

The next morning as the Women's Army moved out towards the town of Darnell, Dar-boo received a message. It read:

*Moo-su must take her army and go find the Men's Armies of The Golden Path. Reason; The men did not return from their mission, "Operation Flood."*

*Operation Flood called for all of The Golden Path tribes' armies to come together as one and go to the Gorilla and Elephant tribes land to launch an attack. The Old Land is very dangerous. Be careful as you enter the Frog Trails. The Council will call for all gangs from The Three Streets to report to the town of Darnell to help in finding our men.*

Dar-boo told Moo-su, Nyrubi and Queen Nstar. "We are powerful together and I'm sure we will do well on our second mission. Yet I still cannot help thinking that something is missing."

Speed-Shay heard what was said and walked over to where they were sitting. Speed-Shay said to them, "Shar-nu, it's Shar-nu who is missing. I was looking forward to talking to her about a lot of things."

Dar-boo looked at Speed-Shay and immediately he knew that she was right, Shar-nu was the missing piece to all of this. He told Moo-su, "I must go to the Tree Patch where Shar-nu lives and bring her with us."

Nyrubi said to Queen Nstar, "I miss my sister. It will be nice to see her again and see if she still wears that strange necklace."

When Shar-nu was a baby girl she was given a wooden key which had a large diamond on the end of it, yet she does not know what or if it locks and unlocks anything.

⊠

Shar-nu was teaching a class about the art on the walls of the water caves to the children that she and her husband Tryumph had devoted their lives to.

General Tryumph came into the classroom and walked up to his wife. He apologized to Shar-nu for the interruption and told her she had some visitors who had come a long way to see her. He then instructed the teaching assistant to take over for Shar-nu.

General Tryumph led Shar-nu over to where she could see all of the ladies and said, "Look!"

Shar-nu looked where her husband pointed and saw a group she immediately recognized as her fellow tribe members. She began to run towards them as Nyrubi, Sebnala and Teela ran toward her. Their hearts were racing and their eyes were full of tears as they finally embraced each other. It was at the Title Holder Games, (which Shar-nu had won), that they had last seen each other and that had been two long years before!

Speed-Shay told Maysheara, "Now we are really as one army. Look at the way they are holding and laughing with each other. I had hoped I would have the honor of meeting Shar-nu." And Maysheara agreed.

Queen Nstar said to the two young Title Holders, "Shar-nu is the kind of woman who would love to talk to you about your training routine and preparations for running."

Dar-boo walked up and hugged Shar-nu. "It has been a while since we all have seen each other, but we are here because—as you can see around you—we have a new army in The Golden Path."

As Shar-nu looked at the new army she said, "It appears the army consists only of women."

Dar-boo said, "In fact, they are the Women's Army of The Golden Path, and they are about to embark on their second mission. However, I do not think we can meet the objective of this mission without you."

Shar-nu was bewildered by what Dar-boo had just said, but first she had to deal with an uneasy feeling that kept creeping into her mind with respect to her father. She asked Nyrubi, "How is our father doing?"

Nyrubi said, "That is our second mission."

Shar-nu said, "What do you mean?"

Sebnala told Shar-nu, "Your father is with all the other Title Holder men and their armies. They went to the Old Land to launch a surprise attack against the Elephant and Gorilla Tribe."

Shar-nu asked, "What's wrong with that?"

Teela said, "They haven't returned. The Council feels something is very wrong with the Title Holder men not returning on time. The Council has called for all gangs from The Three Streets to report to the Council's Army to search for the Men's Army of The Golden Path."

Queen Nstar, Moo-su, Brighthea, Keema, and Graceshell walked up to where Nyrubi, Teela, Sebnala, and Shar-nu were standing so Dar-boo could introduce Shar-nu to them. Most of the Title Holder women had competed against Shar-nu or had see her perform in the Title Holder Games for Shar-nu was known as the fastest woman on The Golden Path, but not for long if Speed-Shay had anything to do with it.

Dar-boo said to Shar-nu, "We must leave at once. The Council's Army has already gone forward through the water caves to get to the Old Land."

Shar-nu told Dar-boo, "I cannot just leave. I am obligated in teaching these children how to read and write, and we were just having a lesson on art and the writings on the water cave walls. My husband, Tryumph, needs me here with the children."

As she spoke, Tryumph walked up and gave Shar-nu a hug, "No, The Golden Path needs you now."

⊠

Shar-nu joined the rest of the Title Holders and the Women's Army as they began their second mission, to find the Title Holder men and assist them in any way possible.

Dar-boo and Keema told the Title Holder women about some of the Gorilla and Elephant Tribes' battle tactics, and how they were known to always use some sort of trickery. Queen Nstar told everyone how Princess Meaira disliked her as well as the tribes of The Golden Path.

Dar-boo said, "There is someone new in the picture who has come back from going to school in the Real World. She is back in the Land of the Seven where she was made Queen by her people, and she is a very smart Plan Master."

Samikia asked, "What's a Plan Master?"

Dar-boo told her, "A 'planmaster' is all the steps you take in order to meet your objective, taking in mind every move and counter move of the other parties involved. If you are very successful in developing plans then you are called 'a Plan Master.' And in the Land of the Seven you cannot do anything without a plan."

⊠

Soon, Moo-su told the Title Holders, "Line the troops up for battle. We will go through the water caves and enter the Frog Trails where unexpected attacks are likely to take place."

As the Women's Army entered the water caves they were all amazed at the writings and art on the walls. Shar-nu told Moo-su, "I have been studying the writings on the wall ever since we searched for Nyrubi."

Shar-nu then looked at Dar-boo and said, "This wall speaks of ten tribes when there are only nine tribes on The Golden Path."

While they were looking at the wall the Women's Army began hearing loud noises, as if they were under attack. Moo-su told her army to prepare, but it was only Prince Donshu of the Wild Boar Tribe.

Prince Donshu told Dar-boo and Moo-su, "The Gorilla and Elephant Tribes are just on the other side of the water cave and they have too many men for us to take without the Men's Armies on our side."

Moo-su told Prince Donshu, "It's too late for my army to move back out of the water cave so we must stand and hold our position." Moo-su told her army, "I know you all are thinking we are outnumbered, but I'd rather fight here then fight running, so prepare your armies for battle."

Shar-nu was standing by the wall when Handfuria noticed the key on her neck was shaking and the diamond was glowing. Dar-boo rushed over to her, "Now I know what was missing! The key to the water gate, and that's just what that key on your neck is. You must be near the secret opening for the key to react."

Nyrubi yelled, "Hurry! They are coming up on us fast. We will hold them off until you find the hidden gate."

Dar-boo and Shar-nu started reading the wall and then Dar-boo said, "Quickly, move a little to the right."

Shar-nu was standing against the wall, and the Gorilla and Elephant Tribes were getting close. Then where Shar-nu was standing a great light came out from behind her.

Dar-boo said to Moo-su, "Shar-nu is the whole key, for it does not work without her."

As the water gates began to open Teela and Keema began yelling to the other troops, "Get your troops through the water gate that Shar -nu has opened!"

The last three people to go through the water gate were Teela, Shar-nu and Dar-boo.

The armies of the Gorilla and Elephant Tribe had been given strict instructions to kill Dar-boo the Peace Keeper on sight. As Dar-boo was entering the water gate tunnel, a member of the Elephant Tribe recognized him and launched an arrow toward him. From the look of it the arrow was right on target to kill Dar-boo when Teela stepped in the way. Dar-boo grabbed Teela as she fell into his arms, then Dar-boo looked at Teela and asked her, "Why, why did you do that?"

Teela looked at him and asked Dar-boo if he would take care of her daughter, Olamae, for her. Dar-boo promised Teela he would.

Queen Nstar grabbed Dar-boo and Baby Olamae. The water gate closed as they ran through it.

⊠

Both the Women's Army and the Wild Boar Tribe's army had made it behind the secret gate.

Queen Nstar told Nyrubi, Sebnala and Shar-nu what had happened to their Teela. "She saved Dar-boo's life. For that she will always be remembered as a heroine. We, the members of The Golden Path, will honor this day forever."

Dar-boo walked over to Sebnala and raised Baby Olamae over his head. "This little baby girl is universal, meaning she is from all the tribes of The Golden Path. Everyone will have a part in raising Baby Olamae."

⊠

Moo-su told all the Title Holders, "This is a whole new place. None of us are familiar with it. We must work and trust in each other to get through this tunnel for we do not know where the tunnel leads."

The Women's Army and the Wild Boar Tribe's Army were working their way through the water gate's secret tunnel. At the same time the Council and their own army along with the gangs of The Three Streets and the 49er Women were making their way through the Frog Trails to the Real Sea Mountains after coming under attack time-after-time by the Elephant and Gorilla Tribes. Ironically, the Frog Trails are directly above the water gate's secret tunnels.

⊠

Queen Elitcal was waiting for two Game Hunters to return from the Real World with the great news that the Real World wanted the men of The Golden Path for slaves. That news would complete her plan. The men would set sail and never again be seen in this life by their wives, women, children or anyone on The Golden Path.

Dar-boo knew they would have to do something fast, but so much was happening it was hard to think. So he kept walking with the Women's Army and the army of the Wild Boar Tribe. He noticed there was not one word being passed among them. It was as if they all realized for the first time that this was not a game, it was for real.

Meanwhile the Council's Army had chosen the right side trail, which runs right over the servant's tunnel, where the Women's Army was at that point.

While fighting their way through the right side of the Frog Trails the 49er Women who had gone with the Council's Army to find the men of The Golden Path captured some of the Elephant Tribe's soldiers. Tozara made them tell where the men of The Golden Path were and if they are still alive.

The soldiers who were captured told Tozara, "We did not want to waste our lives fighting the men of The Golden Path, and our Queen thought it would be less of a risk for our tribe if we tricked your men.

There's nothing you can do. Your men are all captive on a ship bound for the Real World to be sold as slaves."

The Council thanked Tozara and the 49er Women for the way they defeated the Gorilla and Elephant tribes on the Frog Tails right side.

After the battle of the Frog Tails the Council swears the gang and the 49er Women will get equal rights with those who live in a Village or a town.

What that means is The Three Streets can vote to be a Village or a town of The Golden Path once this matter at hand is over and The Golden Path is once again safe.

The Council warned their army and the volunteer fighters from The Three Streets that they knew not what was waiting for them at the end of the tail, but for the night we will eat and rest until sunrise then whatever comes our way we will destroy, for we must get to our men who are being captured by the Elephant and Gorilla Tribes.

Down below the right side of the Frog Tail in the secret tunnel the Women's Army and the army of the Wild Boar tribe were celebrating both the lives of Teela and her newborn daughter Olamae as the soldiers of both armies evaluated what took place in the water cave, moreover how determined The Elephant and Gorilla tribes were when they attacked them in the water cave.

Up where the Title Holders were eating dinner, Prince Donshu asked Shar-nu, "How long have you had the key?"

Shar-nu told Prince Donshu, "I do not know, but as long as I can remember it's been there."

Dar-boo walked over to where Shar-nu was sitting. Then he said, "The key on her neck opens up two gates: one is the water gate, the other is the gate to the Sea Lock. Where the key came from and who might need the Sea Lock are mysteries unto themselves."

Speed-Shay asked Shar-nu if she had ever tried to use the key. Shar -nu answered, "No, but I knew it was special so I never took it off my neck."

Speed-Shay and Shar-nu talked all night about the children Shar-nu worked with and how Shar-nu had won all the races.

The next day came and the Women's Army along with the Wild Boar army were at the end of the tunnel when they heard the marching of another army. Moo-su told her army to prepare for battle quietly. At the same time above the secret tunnel the Council and the gangs of The Three Streets were coming out of the Frog Tails. The Council thought they heard some movement directly beneath where they were standing.

As the armies come face-to-face, they were prepared for a battle to the end. Both sides realized they were all from The Golden Path yet just as they would have liked to tell each other what took place in the Old Land so far, Moo-su, the Wild Boar Tribe and the Council's Army along with the gangs of The Three Streets noticed they were surrounded. It wasn't the Elephant or Gorilla Tribe, it was a tribe that had been unknown to any of the tribes from The Golden Path or the tribes from the Old Land .

Dar-boo told Moo-su, "This is the unknown tribe. I heard of there being a lost tribe but I thought nothing of it at the time."

"This is the lost tribe of the Sharks," Nyrubi said with Shar-nu standing right behind her.

Moo-su commanded all of the armies of The Golden Path to stand down. She wanted to talk to the Shark Tribe's leader, but as she walked toward the unknown tribe she heard someone yell, "Stay where you are!" The unknown tribe got their army in position to attack.

Moo-su and the Council were getting their armies ready for a counterattack when the unknown Shark Tribe noticed something about Shar-nu as she got her troop in attack formation. Shar-nu felt the key around her neck begin shaking, then out from nowhere a huge man shoutsed, "Stop!" Suddenly the unknown Shark Tribe fell to their knees and bowed down to Shar-nu!

Queen Nstar told everyone to wait as the man from the unknown Shark Tribe walked up to Shar-nu and Dar-boo. He asked Shar-nu, "Where did you get that key on your neck? Who are you?"

Shar-nu jumped down from her horse and asked the man, "Who are you?"

Dar-boo asked the man, "Are you the leader of your tribe?"

The man replied, "No."

Then out of nowhere another man said, "I am the leader, and that is my son." The man walked to the front.

The leader of the Shark Tribe was huge. He said to Shar-nu "I am the Czar of the Shark Tribe, and I gave that key to my big sister when we were little. My big sister's name was Gela. And we miss her. She has been gone ever since my tribe voted not to move to The Golden

Path like the other tribes of the Old Land did some years ago. My tribe voted to move near the Real Sea. We also voted to study a new animal so that we could take up a new name and be unknown to the Land of the Seven. We went underground and have lived in secret tunnels for some ninety-eight years," said Czar Sharkaydo.

Shar-nu told the leader of the Shark Tribe, "Czar Sharkaydo, the lady who you speak of, Gela, is my mother."

Czar Sharkaydo walked up to Shar-nu and gave her a huge hug. Then he said to Shar-nu, "I am your uncle. You have a lot of family to meet."

Shar-nu said, "Thank you. I look forward to meeting them all, but first Sir Czar Sharkaydo..."

He stopped her and said, "Please, you can call me uncle."

Shar-nu said, "Yes Uncle, I would like you to meet my family and my fellow members of The Golden Path. This is my sister Nyrubi and my Cousin Sebnala. Then we have General Moo-su, Queen Nstar, Council of The Golden Path, Prince Donshu, Dar-boo The Peace Keeper, and Tozara, leader of The 49er Women. Everyone please meet my uncle Czar Sharkaydo of the Shark Tribe."

Czar Sharkaydo said to everyone, "I am glad to meet you. If you are family to Shar-nu then you are also family to us, and we welcome you all as well. I would like Shar-nu to meet more of her family that she has never seen before. I would be honored if all of you would join us for dinner."

"Dar-boo, the other member of the Council needs to speak to you about a situation that happened in the Frog Tails," said Prince Donshu as they watched the Shark Tribe welcome home Shar-nu.

Moo-su said to Czar Sharkaydo, "We are truly grateful, but we are on a mission. We have some new information we need to discuss, so I do not think we would be great guests for your dinner right now."

Czar Sharkaydo said to Moo-su, "Sure you will and you can discuss this matter over dinner. Come and let your armies get some much needed rest."

After the armies got themselves ready for dinner, the Council told Moo-su what great fighters the 49er Women were and how the 49er Women captured some soldiers from the Elephant Tribe and made them divulge the plan to do away with the men of The Golden Path.

While at dinner Shar-nu met all of her family she had never known. It also gave people of The Golden Path some time to get to know each other. Tozara wanted very much to speak with the other Title Holders.

Tozara told them about the Elephant Tribe's plans and how they planned to use the Real Sea to get rid of the men of The Golden Path. Dar-boo was amazed at the plan of the Elephant and Gorilla Tribe, and how they used the Real Sea to their advantage. None of the Tribes from The Golden Path were familiar with large bodies of water. This was all new to them.

Prince Donshu said to the other Title Holder Men and Women, "Our armies are not equipped for a battle at sea. We are trained for battle on land only. What do we do?"

Tozara said to everyone, "Whatever we do, we must move quickly. The captured soldier told me some people called the Game Hunters will be returning from the Real World to sail far away with our men so they can be sold as slaves."

The Council said to the members of The Golden Path, "We should prepare our armies to launch out after the Elephant and Gorilla Tribes at once."

Moo-su said to the Council, "I think it would be wise to think through a plan together before we try to attack on unfamiliar land. How are we going to attack those things that stand up in the water?"

Tozara told Moo-su, "Those things in the water are called 'ships,' and they are used for transporting by water."

Czar Sharkaydo told Dar-boo he had studied Dar-boo's Great Grandfather Comboos' philosophy. "Comboos was a great man. He made the rules of The Golden Path, he envisioned The Golden Path having a Council which is now at my table, eating dinner with my tribe. Moreover he was a true genius for making the Title Holder Games one of the rules."

Dar-boo thanked Czar Sharkaydo saying, "I am truly grateful for that compliment."

Nyrubi asked Shar-nus's uncle what his favorite food was. He replied , "Crab, lobster and halibut."

Samikia asked, "How does your tribe catch the crab, lobsters and halibut?"

Czar Sharkaydo told her, "We have learned over the years how to make fishing boats. My tribe has now become somewhat expert in the craft of making boats."

Dar-boo said, "I have been doing some studying of my own about the key on Shar-nu's neck, and I have found that her key unlocks two doors that have been closed for a very long time."

Czar Sharkaydo went on to say, "We had no need for the water gate to be open, yet the other gate that the key unlocks is very important to us. It is the key to unlock the Sea Lock gates. You see we could not defend ourselves by sea, so we voted on making an army that could fight on the sea. Along with making fishing ships we started making ships that we could us to help defend us from attack by sea.

"We haven't been able to use our defense ships because they have been locked behind the Sea Lock gates for some twenty years. That is when my sister left the tribe with the key. That was one of the main reasons we decided to move to the Real Sea and become unknown to the rest of the tribes."

Czar Sharkaydo said to Dar-boo, "The generals of my water army are excited about Shar-nu's return with the key of the locks. Our Grandfathers were generals in the first water army, but they were killed when our fighting ships were stuck behind the Sea Lock gates. Once the Sea Lock gates are opened again my tribe can give decent burials to our men who did not make it out alive. We must do that before we move our fighting ships out of the Sea Lock."

Sebnala asked Czar Sharkaydo, "So you think your fighting ships are still functional after such a long period of time? Could they be used in battle if needed?"

"The ships that my tribe build can stand the test of time. Yes, if I must say so myself," said Czar Sharkaydo. "At the next sunrise we shall open the Sea Lock gates for the first time in twenty years and finally see what has become of our battleships. Now enough of this talk! I wish to talk about my lovely niece and the rest of the members of The Golden Path," Czar Sharkaydo shouted out to his guests.

Moo-su felt everyone should relax and enjoy themselves so she asked Czar Sharkaydo if he could have some of his people play music. Then Moo-su said to Czar Sharkaydo, "May we present to you the newest member of The Golden Path, Baby Olamae?"

"I would be honored," said Czar Sharkaydo.

Moo-su did not tell Czar Sharkaydo what had happened to the men of The Golden Path, for she thought Shar-nu needed to get to know her family and her new tribe. The problem was for the members of The Golden Path to resolve. So Moo-su told all of the members to keep what was going on with their men quiet and that they would leave first thing in the morning. You could not tell by looking at Moo-su but she was very worried about whether they had sufficient time to save the mens' lives.

The Council said to Moo-su, "We can attack from land, but we are no good when it comes to the water."

Dar-boo said to Prince Donshu, "We must get our armies positioned where the capture ship enters and departs the mountain into the sea. That will be our last chance to free our men."

Dar-boo told Moo-su to take the Women's Army along with Tozara and the 49er Women and find out where the Elephant and Gorilla Tribes headquarters were, then destroy them.

Moo-su asked the Council if the mission called for the death of the two tribal leaders, Queen Elitcal and Princess Meaira. The Council replied, "No, our first priority is to free our men and make sure that this can never happen again. We will deal with the two leaders in accordance with our laws of war. They will be brought to justice."

Dar-boo said to all of the Title Holders, "We must reach the two borders before the the capture ship sails with our men to the Real World."

Nyrubi said, "I know we have overcome a lot, and I know we are to believe in ourselves and the members of The Golden Path. I do. But I have got to say our plan might not be a match for the Elephant and Gorilla's plan, and I am not ashamed to ask for help if needed. I have to say this. I think you all are wrong when you say we should not tell the Shark Tribe or Shar-nu about the situation with our men."

The Council said to Nyrubi, "How dare you say that we are wrong. Do you know what that means?"

Then Moo-su said, "I think she is right. We should take a vote on the matter of whether we should seek help from the Shark Tribe."

Brighthea told the members of The Golden Path, "I do not think this is a voting matter, for we all know we do not have an army that can fight on water. Moreover to think we somehow can get to the two leaders of the Elephant and Gorilla Tribes before they send our men away is wishful thinking. I'm with Nyrubi. We must face reality: we, the mighty tribes of The Golden Path, are in a situation that we are totally ill equipped to deal with. There is no shame in asking for help. The shame is to have too much pride to admit we need help and risk losing our men forever."

The members of The Golden Path voted on asking the Shark Tribe for assistance in locating the men of The Golden Path, bringing them home safely and destroying once and for all the Elephant and Gorilla Tribes.

The Council asked Dar-boo, "Now that we have voted on seeking help from the Shark Tribe to find our men how do we go about asking for help? Never have we the tribes of The Golden Path been in a position such as the one we are faced with right now."

Queen Nstar said to Dar-boo, "We must tell Shar-nu everything about where our men are. Then we must send her with the members of the Lion Tribe, along with Baby Olamae, to speak with her uncle, Czar Sharkaydo.

"She must tell Czar Sharkaydo what we've been through and why we used the secret tunnel. Then ask Czar Sharkaydo if they would assist us or join in fighting the Elephant and Gorilla Tribes and getting our men back safely." Queen Nstar went on to say, "He will want the word of the Peace Keeper to speak for all of The Golden Path. Dar-boo, you must inform him of how important it is that we get our men back. Stress to him that if they could so boldly plot against us then surely his tribe would be next."

Dar-boo told the Council, "We must be ready to attack at sunrise. It would be advantageous to have the Shark Tribe's help, but it has been over twenty years since the Shark Tribe has even seen their fighting ships. They must need time to retrain and assess their fighting ships. We cannot ask them to put themselves in harm's way if they are not battle ready. I fear that by the time they will be ready it will be too late to save our men.

"If Shar-nu wishes to stay with her new family, it's OK with me, but we will finish off the Elephant and Gorilla for good. So everyone get as much rest as you can for tomorrow. We will be needing it," said Dar-boo.

⊠

Back at the sea view the Elephant and Gorilla Tribe leaders, Queen Elitcal and Princess Meaira, prepared to pay a little visit to the captured men of The Golden Path.

"The men will be furious when they learn they have been fooled by women. They will want to know why didn't we just kill them instead of going through all of this trouble."

Princess Meaira said to Queen Elitcal, "The Game Hunters will return tomorrow and the men of The Golden Path will be gone for good. Why do I have a feeling you are still not satisfied with the outcome?"

Queen Elitcal told Princess Meaira how she'd been working on this plan all of her life, anticipating the moment she would come face-to-face with one person and one person only. "I can't wait to see his face when he learns he has been captured by me," said Queen Elitcal. "I know that as long as he is alive the possibility exists for something to go very wrong. But by now that person should be done with."

"Who might that person be that you are speaking about?" asked Princess Meaira.

Queen Elitcal replied, "I speak of The Peace Keeper of The Golden Path, Dar-boo."

Seeing the men of The Golden Path being held against their will should have been very enjoyable, however, instead Queen Elitcal received a piercing blow. Dar-boo was not among the captured. In fact she received a communiqué saying that there was another army of The Golden Path and they were with Dar-boo. It went on to say that when they went to attack that army they had disappeared like magic.

Queen Elitcal began shouting at the soldier, "You had a chance to kill Dar-boo and you missed him!"

Then Queen Elitecal said to Princess Meaira, "Send your army to seek and destroy this so-called Women's Army. You'll be in perfect position to go head-to-head with Queen Nstar, who is your lifelong adversary."

"This so-called Women's Army is not in the Frog Tails and they have not been spotted anywhere in the Old Land. So where could they be?" asked Princess Meaira.

Queen Elitcal said flatly, "There is nowhere they could have hidden. Nevertheless, we do not know where they are. For all we know they could be right outside our territory. That is why it is crucial that we find this new army of The Golden Path for they are the men's last chance."

Queen Elitcal also told Princess Meaira, "If you find any opportunity to take Dar-boo out, then do it. Do not spend your time looking for Queen Nstar until you have killed Dar-boo the Peace Keeper."

Princess Meaira said, "What and how I feel about Queen Nstar is far less important then the plan that you so skillfully planned and executed. If this plan calls for the Peace Keeper to die, then it shall be done."

Queen Elitcal asked Princess Meaira, "Who is the leader of the new Women's Army of The Golden Path, and what is he like? Unlike the research I have done on Dar-boo, I did not put in much study on the others of The Golden Path."

Princes Meaira said, "I too am guilty of focusing on only one person instead of studying all of the members of The Golden Path. This is the one thing I fear may come back to haunt us in the end.

"Let's move this plan forward to sunrise to go and meet the two Game Hunters so they can sail east into the Real Sea. Then we will sail west."

⊠

The night before Shar-nu unlocked the Sea lock doors, Sebnala was still up because baby girl Olamae was crying and would not go back to sleep. Sebnala was not the only one to hear Baby Olamae crying. Sebnala was holding her little niece when Aqualeen entered the room.

Aqualeen is the wife of Czar Sharkaydo. Aqualeen is five months pregnant and very infatuated with Baby Olamae. She was in awe of the way everyone pitched in to help take care of the baby. Aqualeen said to Sebnala, "Where is the baby's mother?" Then she said quickly to Sebnala, "Oh! I'm very sorry for prying. You do not need to tell me anything. That may be why you have been crying. I will leave you alone now."

Sebnala said to Aqualeen, "Please stay."

Aqualeen stayed. Sebnala proceeded to tell her what had happened over the last three months. She told her what had happened to Olamae's mother. The two women talked all night about The Golden Path and how the Shark Tribe became a secret tribe. They talked about how the Shark Tribe kept the tribes of The Golden Path from knowing they even existed.

Aqualeen told Sebnala she had heard of a girl that was from the Land of the Seven when she was in school in the Real World. They attended the same college in the Real World. "The girl I had heard of was outgoing and very smart. She loved beating men at their own games for fun. She soon found herself alone; no one wanted to be around her because she was so obsessed with betting and beating men in anything and everything.

"Before she came back to the Land of the Seven we went head-to-head in an event. I won and she was a sore loser for she does not like to lose to anyone male or female. Her name was Elitcal.

I wonder if she could be behind the plan to do away with the men of The Golden Path."

Aqualeen asked Sebnala if she could hold Baby Olamae. Sebnala handed the baby over to her saying, "But of course, you may."

Sebnala began telling Aqualeen how very much they missed their men. Aqualeen asked Sebnala pointedly, "Who is it you miss most?"

Sebnala said, "I miss a man named Leo-Pual. He is a General in the powerful Lion Tribe. When he was a little boy, he lost his father and mother in a flood. Our King Zhaun found him in the water and raised him up as his own son. Leo-Pual, like all of the men of the Lion Tribe, is very strong.

"Never before have they been in a situation like this one, and what bothers me most is that I do not know if our men of The Golden Path would even call for their women to help them overcome this situation.

"The men of The Golden Path have way too much pride to seek help from anyone, and it has carried over to the women. We find ourselves needing help but it is difficult to seek help from anyone who does not understand how the tribes of The Golden Path operate and treat its members."

"I know how you feel Sebnala," said Aqualeen. "My tribe had to become unknown if our ancestors wanted to live and work off the Real Sea the way they wanted to. It hurt some in our tribe, as it hurt Shar-nu's mother, not to move to The Golden Path with the rest of the tribes, especially because they always wanted to participate in the Title Holder Games. When they found out that they could not participate in the games, some of them ran away, like Shar-nu's mother. However, they did not run to The Golden Path to be made a slave. They ran to the Real World to go to school. After going to school, a lot of them joined the Navy for four years."

"What is a navy?" asked Sebnala.

Aqualeen said, "A navy is a tactical branch of an army that fights from the water instead of the land. The navy uses huge ships and submarines. You actually live on these ships for months, sometimes years, at a time. I really prefer being on a sub."

Sebnala asked, "What is a sub?"

"A sub is an airtight boat that attacks from underneath the water. The ships that are on top of the water cannot see them."

Sebnala said, "That is amazing! Do you know how to do all of that?"

"Yes," Aqualeen said while holding Baby Olamae. "I am qualified to command a fleet of attack subs if needed."

Sebnala told Aqualeen that her people would be leaving at sunrise to save their men. She continued, "I cannot help but think that even if we defeat the Elephant and Gorilla Tribes on land we will be unsuccessful in stopping the ship from sailing away with our men. Losing our men would be more devastating then losing to the Elephant and Gorilla Tribes. I realize that your tribe needs time to train and so we could not ask you to come with us. We know how much time it took us to train, so we would not think of asking you to do something that we ourselves would not be ready to do."

Aqualeen asked, "Do you have a plan of attack ready for sunrise?"

"No, not as of yet," Sebnala admitted

Aqualeen said, "I will assist you in going against the Elephant and Gorilla Tribes, but we must have a plan. We will surely lose the battle and your men forever if we go up against the enemy without a strategy.

Sebnala said, "A plan?"

"Yes, a plan. And I am a Plan Master!" said Aqualeen. "There is only one other female Plan Master that I know of, and she uses her plans to dominate. Her name is Queen Elitcal of the Elephant Tribe."

Sebnala said, "What do you think we should do, Aqualeen?"

"Go get all of your army of women and the Title Holder women, but do not bring your leader for they will not approve of my next move."

"What is that?" asked Sebnala.

"That is to open the Sea Lock gate right now instead of in the morning when everyone thinks it will be opened. The third part of my plan is for us to leave a note for your tribe and my tribe to read. The note will tell them that we have gone to attack the Elephant and Gorilla Tribes by the sea, and instruct them to attack by land in order for us to save the men of The Golden Path."

She continued, "Sebnala you need to gather together all of the Title Holder women and some of your army, and I will gather mine. We will meet at the stone wall outside the territory near the Sea Lock. We must also write notes to my husband, Czar Sharkaydo, and your leader of The Golden Path."

Aqualeen told Sebnala, "We need someone to make sure every one of the Title Holder women gets to the stone wall on time."

As she was speaking, the leader of the 49er Women walked into the room to see how Baby Olamae was doing. Sebnala smile and introduced Tozara to Aqualeen.

Sebnala said to Aqualeen, "Maybe Tozara would be just the person to gather all of the Title Holder women and meet you at the stone wall gate as soon as possible."

Aqualeen agreed. "Go and retrieve your tribe members, along with Shar-nu, and meet me outside this room. Hurry, we must act quickly if we are going to open the Sea Lock gates before my tribe wakes up. They are planning an elaborate ceremony to open the Sea Lock gates."

Sebnala said to Aqualeen, "You do not have to do this."

Aqualeen said, "Yes I do, if we are to finally do away with the Elephant and Gorilla Tribes. If they are bold enough to go against the tribes of The Golden Path, then who is to say they would not launch an attack on us next? So I say it would be smart if my tribe joined in the battle against the Gorilla and Elephant Tribes for the betterment of the Land of Seven."

Tozara spoke next, addressing Aqualeen, "Thank you for joining us, to defeat the Elephant and Gorilla Tribes. Now I will go and assemble the Women's Army so that we can meet you on time. Go now and be safe. We must be successful in this mission of saving the men of The Golden Path. Keep in mind ladies, we will not have another shot at this."

⊠

Tozara gathered all of the Women's Armies and they left for the stone wall where they were to meet Aqualeen and the Title Holder women. Sebnala gathered all of the Title Holder women and waited outside of Baby Olamae's room for Aqualeen to return with her own army.

Aqualeen's sea fighting army was also a Women's Army and had been training all of their lives to finally get a chance to run the mighty and powerful sea subs their ancestors had built before they were even born. Aqualeen's army had spent all of their lives studying the sea subs and how to operate them under battle situations. Aqualeen and her army felt blessed to be among those who would see the Sea Lock gates being opened after more than twenty years of being closed.

Aqualeen thought, "Many have come and gone, never knowing when the Sea Lock gates would open again. This is a great day for all the tribes of the Land of the Seven who fight for peace and freedom."

Aqualeen and her first general, General Aliquel, met with all of the Title Holder women except the three leaders, for they would never have approved of this plan. Moo-su, Queen Nstar and Keema were adamant about waiting for Czar Sharkaydo's approval. Aqualeen believed that there was no time for more talk of any kind: they had to act and act now if they were to stand any chance of rescuing the men of The Golden Path.

Just outside Baby Olamae's room Aqualeen and her sea fighting Women's Army met with the Women's Army of The Golden Path. Aqualeen introduced her First General, Aliquel, to the Title Holder women. General Aliquel said to the women, "Before we go any further you must choose your leader. Each leader will give orders to her own army. We are on this mission together but we have different areas of expertise. We will be splitting up after Shar-nu opens the Sea Lock gates."

Sebnala said, "We, the Title Holders of the Women's Army of The Golden Path, have voted and would be honored if Nyrubi would accept the duty of leading in the plan to rescue the men of The Golden Path."

Nyrubi immediately said, "I am the one who is honored, and I do accept the role."

Aqualeen proceeded to tell Nyrubi the plan. "We will split up. Some of you will go with Aliquel and the others will come with me." Nyrubi called out the command for Graceshell, Brighthea, Speed-Shay and Maysheara to go with Aliquel and for Samikia, Handfurya, Sebnala and Shar-nu to follow her and Aqualeen.

Aqualeen then said, "When Shar-nu opens the Sea Lock gates we must act fast in getting to my tribe's warships and subs and getting them out, because we do not know how long the gate will stay open."

Nyrubi with her Title Holder women of The Golden Path along with the Women's sea fighting army of the newly found Shark Tribe led by Aqualeen and her First General Aliquel, were finally on there way to open the Sea Lock gates. They had been walking for some time. As they came over a ridge Aliquel abruptly stopped. She pointed and said excitedly to Samikia, "Look, there it is!" It was the Sea Lock, and the gate that needed to be opened was right in the middle of it.

While both Women's Armies walked toward the Sea Lock gates, Aqualeen instructed Nyrubi and Shar-nu on how exactly to open the doors. She told the women, "In order for the key to open the Sea Lock gates, Shar-nu must go to the top and place the key in the hole. The hole will widen. Do not worry for if the person who opens the Sea Lock gates is 'true' the key will forbid him or her to fall in. However, if the person attempting to open the gate is not 'true' then that person will be sucked in to the keyhole. In addition to that, the key itself will be sucked into the keyhole never to be used again. In other words this is our only opportunity to open the Sea Lock gates."

They all stood frozen in front of the place that the Shark Tribe called "the Sea Lock." Aqualeen told Shar-nu and Nyrubi, "When the doors open the members of my tribe and myself will dive into the water and swim towards out fighting subs. We must get the fighting subs up and running and through the Sea Lock gates into the Real Sea before the doors close. Shar-nu, if you do not wish to do this, now is the time to say so, for the doors of the Sea Lock can only be opened by you."

Shar-nu said, "For the love of my land, tribes, and The Golden Path, this must be done. We have lost a great member of The Golden Path, Teela, and she would not want to stop until the mission of freeing our men from the hands of the Elephant and Gorilla Tribes is complete. So this must be done." Shar-nu looked back at all the Title Holder women while walking toward the top of the Sea Lock, to stand near the keyhole which opens the doors.

Nyrubi said to Sebnala and Aqualeen,"This is it. Only time will tell if the Sea Lock gates will open for Shar-nu."

Sebnala yelled, "Shar-nu, you can do it!"

Brighthea also yelled, "I know you can do this! Just believe in yourself Shar-nu."

Shar-nu looked at both of the Women's Armies and shouted, "For The Golden Path!" Then she placed the key in the keyhole.

Everything started to shake as Shar-nu turned the key. Then Aliquel said to Aqualeen, "Look!" The Sea Lock gates began to slightly open, but for some reason the doors would not open enough to fit the fighting sub through them.

Handfurya shouted, "You're doing great Shar-nu!"

Then the rest of the Women's Armies began to shout encouragements. The keyhole suddenly got much larger. A bright light came through and shot right to the sky. It lifted Shar-nu into the air. Nyrubi rushed up to Shar-nu and grabbed her hand, which made the Sea Lock gates jar open a few inches more but Shar-nu began looking tired. The keyhole began pulling Shar-nu into it when Sebnala handed Baby Girl Olamae to Aliquel and ran up the Sea Lock walls to reach for Nyrubi's hand. The three women holding onto each other made Shar-nu rise up and the gate open just a little more. The keyhole was powerful, and its pulling force was taking a toll on Shar-nu. The doors began to close and it looked as though Shar-nu was about to be sucked into the keyhole. Aliquel ran up to where Shar-nu, Sebnala and Nyrubi were and handed the baby to Sebnala as all of the members of the Lion Tribe held on to Shar-nu. Suddenly it began to storm; thunder and lightning bolts began to fly. A lightning bolt hit the Sea Lock gates with incredible force. Aqualeen started jumping up and down with joy and happiness because the gate was opening.

The Shark Tribe got ready to dive into the water. The keyhole closed and Shar-nu fell to the ground near Nyrubi, Sebnala, and Baby Girl Olamae. Graceshell and Brighthea rushed to get them down from the Sea Lock walls. Nyrubi watched as the Shark Tribe dove into the sea to go retrieve the fighting subs that their grandmothers had made and they had studied all of their lives.

Nyrubi told all of the members of The Golden Path, "We have done all that we can do. Now we must wait for the Shark Tribe's Women's Army to return from the Sea Lock with their fighting subs."

The Title Holder women from The Golden Path waited patiently for the women of the Shark Tribe to return with their warships. It had already been over seven minutes, and they had not yet made it into their four ships. They still had to get into the ships, start them up and maneuver them out of the Sea Lock gates successfully.

Samikia said to Speed-Shay, "I am going in." But Speed-Shay grabbed her arm and said, "I know that you want to help, but we of The Golden Path do not know how to swim. Surely you will die if you jump into that water." Just then the Title Holders of The Golden Path began to see the subs of the Shark Tribe approach from the Sea Lock. It was an amazing moment for the women of both armies.

Aqualeen came out of the subs and said to Nyrubi, "We must hurry before the men of my tribe come to open the Sea Lock themselves. Now Nyrubi, you know what the plan is: command your army into the subs, for we still must meet Tozara along with the 49er

Women and the Women's Army of The Golden Path at the stone wall. Then we will launch an all-out water attack against the Elephant and Gorilla Tribes. It will be a battle they will never forget."

Aqualeen also told Nyrubi, "We will be taking two fishing ships, one for the men when we destroy the ships they are on, and one for the fire ship. We'll run it into the captured men's ship to give us time to help your men onto our ship successfully without any injuries or casualties."

Aqualeen told Shar-nu and Nyrubi about the one water war that had taken place in the Real World between the English and the Vikings along with Eric the Red. "They would use fire ships for defense, but sometimes for offense as well. We will be using the fire ship for offense."

Samikia made sure all of the Title Holders were on their assigned subs and then told Nyrubi who on each sub was in charge of the Title Holder women from The Golden Path, since they had gone to rescue their men without their real leaders who were Moo-su, Keema, Queen Nstar, Dar-boo and the Commander of The Golden Path, Prince Donshu of the Wild Boar Tribe. The Title Holder women of The Golden Path knew this was disobedience, but they believed they did not have enough time to wait for the Sea Lock gates ceremony and the Shark Tribe's Men's Army.

In the Shark Tribe, the women train to be in charge of the water fighting subs. The warships were reserved exclusively for the men of the Shark Tribe, yet one warship came out from behind the Sea Lock gates. Someone had started this warship even though they were not given the order by Aqualeen.

Everyone was filled with joy at the sight of the ships. Some were seeing them for the first time in nearly twenty years. The excited women were laughing and talking all at once but suddenly everyone was silent. They were astounded by the sight of the warship coming from behind the Sea Lock gates. Then Aliquel came out of the warship and said to everyone, "Remember this moment forever.

"We are all happy at this moment, however, we have no idea what lies ahead for our two great Women's Armies. We do not know their weapons of choice, but what we do know is that the men of The Golden Path need our assistance right now and they will be rescued by any means necessary. No, I should not have taken the men's warship, but for some reason I have a gut feeling we will be needing this warship in saving the men of The Golden Path from the capture ship they have been placed on. We also needed this ship in case the capture ships themselves are equipped with weapons of war.

Aqualeen looked at Aliquel and said, "You have broken the lifetime agreement between the men and women of the Shark Tribe regarding the warships and subs. Women are not allowed to operate the warships, only the subs. This rule has stood solid for over one hundred years and you will pay dearly for that decision. But now is not the time. Take the warship and the fire boat to the Real Sea. They will not see the subs and will assume that those boats are our only defense. Then I will launch a surprise attack from underneath their boat and destroy them."

Aqualeen then said to the whole group, "There is no turning back now. We all are in this to win together, so when we get out to the Real Sea and into the water battle I expect every one of you to perform exactly as you have been trained. I believe that if you do that we have a great chance of being successful in this mission and saving the men of The Golden Path."

Then both Women's Armies went forward towards the Real Sea, not knowing if they would ever see their men of the Shark Tribe or the men of The Golden Path again.

⊠

The next morning came and it was time for the unlocking of the Sea Lock gates ceremony.

Moo-su, Dar-boo, Queen Nstar and the other members of The Golden Path all joined Czar Sharkaydo and his Shark Tribe's Water Fighting Army for breakfast. Czar Sharkaydo noticed that some of the members of The Golden Path were missing and asked Moo-su, "Where is that lovely baby girl Olamae? I was looking forward to seeing her face."

Moo-su and Queen Nstar looked around and confirmed that many of the Title Holder women along with other members of the army were missing.

Then Keema asked Czar Sharkaydo, "Where is your lovely wife Aqualeen? It seems many men are without their wives this fine morning."

Then Dar-boo stood up and said to Czar Sharkaydo, "Something is very wrong here. There are no women present at the breakfast table."

That is when Queen Nstar said to everyone, "They left on their own this morning."

Prince Donshu started laughing and said to Czar Sharkaydo, "I did not think they had it in them to want to be on their own."

Moo-su was furious with the Title Holder women but Czar Sharkaydo said, "Do not worry. They will wait for us to arrive at the Sea Lock gates so we can all be there when the gate opens. Then we will pull all our battleships out from behind the gates together. We will start the ceremonies directly after we eat breakfast so do not worry about the women right now. Go on, let's eat for today is a very special day for my tribe. We have not seen our tribe's battleships since my grandfather was the Czar of the Shark Tribe. Furthermore, when my father was Czar he never saw the battleships that were behind the Sea Lock gates, so I will be looking up to the sky for their guidance when the Sea Lock gates are finally opened. Even though we have to save the men from The Golden Path this is still a good thing for our tribes to come together for one cause."

As Czar Sharkaydo led his people to the Sea Locks to start the ceremony he again asked Moo-su where his niece Shar-nu was because none of this could happen without her. Moo-su replied to Czar Sharkaydo , "By the time we arrive at the Sea Lock they should be there, for they all know about the ceremony which takes place after breakfast."

The tribes of The Golden Path and the Shark Tribe were very near the Seal locks when General Kenray of the Shark Tribe's Water Fighting Army began running toward the Sea Lock. He yelled to the others, "It's open already! The gates are already opened." Everyone from the Land of the Seven rushed over to see for themselves if what the general said was true.

Czar Sharkaydo said, "The gates could only be opened by one person and one gate key and that person is Shar-nu. What this means is the women from all of our tribes think they are equipped to complete this mission on their own. I am so disappointed in my wife Aqualeen for she is responsible for this! I must apologize for this defiance and ask for your forgiveness, Moo-su and Dar-boo."

That's when the Council said to Czar Sharkaydo, "No apology is necessary for we do not see it that way. We see it as the love of women toward the men they all love so much, and when it comes to your loved ones there is nothing you will not do to help in any way possible. Furthermore we are proud of the Title Holder women and your wife Aqualeen for taking charge and going on their own to save the men of The Golden Path. We have come to the understanding that a woman's intuition is to be taken very seriously. They did know how monumental this ceremony was to be for your tribe and yet they must have deeply believed that time was of the essence and action had to be taken now not later.

"It is not easy to feel confident in doing something and going somewhere you have never been before. So that is a compliment to all of us here for the women we all helped train into true warriors. So let us begin the task of retrieving all of the Shark Tribe's warships from behind the Sea Lock gates that Shar-nu successfully opened early this morning. Now, lets sit down and start figuring out our plan to assist in the mission of saving the men of The Golden Path, moreover making sure the Women's Armies of both tribes are equipped to go into battle with the Elephant and the Gorilla tribes."

The plan they came up with and agreed upon was for the two gangs of The Three Streets—the Dark Rangers and the Village Diggers—to try to stop the ship holding the men of The Golden Path. They were to prevent it from getting out to the Real Sea. The plan also called for Prince Donshu and the Wild Boar Tribe's armies to wait on shore for any of the Elephant or Gorilla Tribe members who might try to return from the sea.

Czar Sharkaydo said to Moo-su, "Who will be coming with me and my Water Fighting Army on the warships? And who will go with my land army to attack the headquarters of the Elephant and Gorilla Tribes?"

Moo-su told Czar Sharkaydo, "I wish for Queen Nstar and Dar-boo to go with you. Keema along with the Council's Army and I will attack where the leaders of the Elephant and Gorilla Tribes lay their heads at night.

"The reason I wish for Queen Nstar and Dar-boo to go with you is because if the leaders of the enemy tribes sees either of these two they will abort their original plan and resolve to assassinate both Queen Nstar and Dar-boo as their first priority.

"We do not want to change this mission into a war about Dar-boo and Queen Nstar. We will stay with our original mission to destroy both of those tribes once and for all. This will also be a warning to any other tribe never to launch a surprise attack against The Golden Path."

Czar Sharkaydo said, "I respect your decision and now it is time to start the mission of saving the men of The Golden Path."

One of the Shark Tribe soldiers ran up to Czar Sharkaydo and told him, "One of the men's warships is missing. That means the women of our tribe have broken one of our rules, which is that the warships are for the men only and the subs are for the women."

Czar Sharkaydo looked at the Council of The Golden Path, then he told the soldier, "Now is not the time to be worried about broken rules. Now is the time for helping our fellow tribe members complete the objective of saving the men of The Golden Path. Furthermore if my wife Aqualeen felt she needed the warship, then that is that."

Czar Sharkaydo told everyone at the Sea Lock, "We all see what this has come down to. All of our loved ones are involved in this matter with the Elephant and Gorilla Tribes in some way or another, and for that, we the Shark Tribe now declare war on the Elephant Tribe and the Gorilla Tribe.

"I say this to the men of The Shark Tribe, we are going to the Real Sea for the first time in forty-seven years, but just like our fathers before us, we will be great warriors on the sea and on the land. In addition, for the Elephant and Gorilla Tribes making us enter this war in such an unorthodox way they must be shown no mercy, regardless of who they are."

Dar-boo told Czar Sharkaydo, "If it is possible, we would like to capture the leaders of these two tribes and bring them to justice for war crimes committed against all of the tribes of the Land of Seven."

Czar Sharkaydo said, "If there is no more to be said then the men of the Shark Tribe's great army will move out to the Real Sea. I know you all will prove to be the great warriors you have trained so diligently to be all of your lives, and with our superior warships and weapons we are assured the victory in this war. Let's bring our women home as the heroines they are for going ahead on their own to save the men of The Golden Path."

The last thing that Czar Sharkaydo said to Moo-su was, "I am looking forward to meeting the great men of The Golden Path, and I am honored to be a part of the operation to free them and to avenge us all."

Moo-su told Czar Sharkaydo, "I know all of my members of The Golden Path miss their tribes, furthermore, I know when we get through this hard time we will all be much closer to each other. So as you go out to the Real Sea I will pray and thank the Higher Power for your great friendship that I hope will last for the rest of time."

Czar Sharkaydo said to Moo-su, "You and your other members have not troubled anybody and you deserve to be happy and have a great ending to all this madness that the Elephant and Gorilla Tribes have inflicted upon the tribes of The Golden Path. So you go safely and capture the two leaders of the Elephant and Gorilla Tribes. Destroy their armies for good."

As Moo-su was waving good-bye to all of the men on the warships leading out to the Real Sea with some of her members of The Golden Path on board, Queen Nstar called to Moo-su, "Be safe. You are a great leader Moo-su," as they sailed farther and farther away from each other.

So the plan was this, Moo-su and Keema would lead the land attack along with the Council and their army. The Wild Boar Tribe's army along with O'Hally and the two gangs from The Three Streets— the Village Daggers and the Dark Rangers—all came to be of some assistance to both the Women's Army of The Golden Path and of the Shark Tribe to rescue the men of The Golden Path.

⊠

Back at the Sea Palace in the Gorilla and Elephant Tribe's territory, Queen Elitcal finally received the message she had been waiting for since she started this plan. The Game Hunters had been successful. On board the ship with the two game hunters were the men who would serve as auctioneers in selling the Men of The Golden Path to the Real World as slaves. She immediately gave the signal to put the final step of her plan into work.

Queen Elitcal told the soldiers to bring the capture ships to the Real Sea at once so they can be hooked up to the battleship, The *S.S. Rainier* from the Real World.

The *S.S. Rainier* was to tow them to the Real World, where the men from The Golden Path would finally be out of their way. Now we can go to take over The Golden Path and there will be no one to defend it. We will launch this massive attack within two days.

Princess Meaira said to Queen Elitcal, "I do not think we are in the clear just yet, for there is still another army we have not encountered; the Women's Army of The Golden Path. I would feel much more confident if our army would have finished them off in the water caves, instead of allowing them to disappear into thin air."

Queen Elitcal told Princess Meaira, "Do not worry yourself over small things. For one, none of the tribes from The Golden Path can swim, so even if they were to try to intervene to save their men they will be on land and their men will be far away from their reach. The Women's Army of The Golden Path is no match for our two armies. If they show up here, we will destroy them for good. It would give us another opportunity to kill Queen Nstar and Dar-boo."

Queen Elitcal and Princess Meaira looked out of the Sea Palace windows overlooking the Real Sea and saw the capture ships being hooked up to the fighting ship the *S.S. Rainier*.

Queen Elitcal told Princess Meaira, "It will not be long before the men of The Golden Path are powerless to stop us from taking over their land."

Princess Meaira and Queen Elitcal begin dancing and shouting, "No more trouble from the men, ever again! No more trouble ..."

They repeated this chant again and again as the ship with the captured men from The Golden Path was finally hooked up and on their way with the *S.S. Rainier* leading them further away from the Land of the Seven, never to be seen or heard of again.

⊠

While the men of The Golden Path were being taken away, King Zhaun and the rest of the men Title Holders were trying for the last time to escape, but once again they were unsuccessful.

Queen Elitcal and Princess Meaira were saying good-bye to the men from The Golden Path for good. Queen Elitcal told members of her tribe, "Let the celebration begin! Bring in the entertainment, the food and the drinks. For this is a glorious occasion!"

Queen Elitcal and Princess Meaira were enjoying themselves when suddenly pandemonium broke loose. A loud noise followed by a violent shaking of the palace interrupted their celebration. Members of the Elephant Tribe rushed into action to cover their queen. One of her generals came running to report to Queen Elitcal that her palace was under attack but she should not be alarmed for they were finding out where the explosion came from and would crush the sad attempt ...

Queen Elitcal walked up to General Elfear and gripped his neck, "Sad attempt? Is this what you call a sad attempt?

"Well I see now what you think does not matter in the case. I do all of the thinking for this tribe, and I think that this sad attempt was very successful. Do you think that General Elfear?"

"Yes, my Queen," he answered.

"What is that?" Princess Meaira shouted to Queen Elitcal as she looked out over the Real Sea.

What they did not know is that while Queen Elitcal and Princess Meaira were enjoying the entertainment and lunch the battleships from the Real World were under attack by ships that had appeared out of nowhere. It was the first wave of attacks that would play a part in saving the men from The Golden Path.

Queen Elitcal walked over to the lookout and what she and the Princess saw was like nothing they had ever seen before. It was a war on the Real Sea. Queen Elitcal, along with her tribe and Princess Meaira were in awe and speechless. All of this was new to them. No one from the Land of the Seven even knew that a war could be fought on water.

Queen Elitcal was surprised by the skill of the unknown warships and their capabilities in battle with the battleships from the Real World. "I cannot help the ships from the Real World. I have done my part," said Queen Elitcal. Just as her tribe was coming out of shock, they found themselves under attack. It was Moo-su and Keema leading the charge against the Sea Palace.

Princess Meaira said to Queen Elitcal, "I see their one battleship along with the one fire boat that hit one of the Real World's ships, but where is the other attack against the Real World battleships coming from?"

Queen Elitcal was looking at the battle on the Real Sea between the battleships from the Real World and the warship and subs from the Shark Tribe along with Dar-boo and Queen Nstar on board.

Princess Meaira kept on asking Queen Elitcal, "Where are the other attacks coming from?"

The two leaders of the Elephant and Gorilla Tribes watched helplessly as another battleship from the Real World was sunk by the one warship from the mysterious water warriors, whose identify was yet unknown to Queen Elitcal and Princess Meaira.

Queen Elitcal noticed something sticking out of the water. She rushed over to one of her Guards and said to him, "Take a boat out to the *S.S. Rainier* and tell the captain of the ship the attacks against them are not just coming from the one warship, but from under the water as well. Go now!"

Princess Meaira said to Queen Elitcal, "How could that be? Is it a monster underneath the water who is on the side of the unknown water fighters?"

Queen Elitcal said to Princess Meaira, "Those are no monsters. Those are what the Real World calls submarines. Submarines are air- and water- tight ships that can move underwater to go unnoticed. This is definitely something I did not anticipate. It would make all the sense to plan for a water fight with the members of The Golden Path when we know they are strictly land people. They cannot even swim. Where did they get the warships to amass this massive counterattack?" Queen Elitcal was watching the guard she sent give the message to the Real World's battleships. A battleship began launching barrels of explosives into the water to destroy the Shark Tribe's fighting subs.

Aqualeen ordered her fleet of fighting subs to move away from the battleships from the Real World as one of the four subs took a hit from one of the barrels.

Princess Meaira said, "Look Queen Elitcal, there are four of those sub monsters and they look as if they are retreating."

"Good," Queen Elitcal replied. "While the battleships from the Real World handle their business in the water, we must attend to this land attack from the tribes of The Golden Path. This should not be a problem since they are without their men."

Queen Elitcal told one of her Generals, "The enemy is attacking us from the Real Sea Mountains." Then she ordered him to release the water from the dam. "That will wash out whoever is still below, and we will hold off the troops that manage to survive the flood."

Unbeknownst to Queen Elitcal the Council's Army along with the two gangs from The Three Streets had already gained control of the Elephant Tribe's water source.

Queen Elitcal's guard came to her side, "Our Queen, your safety is in jeopardy. We should leave through one of your secret escape tunnels."

Queen Elitcal told him flatly, "I am not running anywhere. I know my plan will be successful. Give it more time. Look out there in the Real Sea. I told you the battleship from the Real World would put an end to this madness once and for all."

"Now three of the four subs and one of the warships are turning around for a second round of attacks," said Princess Meaira.

Queen Elitcal replied, "Even if they do they will surely be destroyed this time."

The Queen's guard again urged their Queen to please leave, for she had to live. He did not want her to be captured. He reminded her,

"The Queen's safety comes first." But she refused to budge, stating that she would not leave her tribe in the middle of a battle and she had to see her plan through.

The guards told their Queen, "Our tribe knows where to meet if an emergency were ever to arise. Come Queen Elitcal, we must go."

"No. Let me be."

Then Queen Elitcal said this to everyone in her quarters, "First I must make sure Dar-boo the Peace Keeper of The Golden Path is with those who try to attack us at this moment. If so he will die."

It was nighttime and the fireworks from the battle on the Real Sea could be seen for miles. The Women's Fighting Army from the Shark Tribe was holding their own, but the battleships from the Real World seemed to be too much for them. Nevertheless, they kept fighting.

Queen Elitcal said "I'm sure they will not last another hour against the battleship from the Real World. Now I need a report from the front line on the land battle."

One of the soldiers said to her, "We are holding them off, but they have more men and women then we expected."

Queen Elitcal replied, "What does that mean?"

The soldier replied, "Nothing, my Queen, nothing."

⊠

Nyrubi, who was out in the Real Sea battle, said to Aqualeen, "You have done enough for the tribes of The Golden Path. Do not jeopardize your Water Fighting Army any further for us. We are truly thankful for everything your tribe did for us, but I must tell you, do not go back a second time. I am not sure your fleet can handle another hit."

Aqualeen looked at Nyrubi and said, "This is good vs. evil, and evil must not win. This is no longer just about your men. It's bigger than that. Therefore, regardless of the loss of life, we must continue this battle and be victorious." Then she commanded her fleet of subs to dive underwater to launch another attack against the battleships from the Real Sea.

⊠

"We are winning in the battle on the Real Sea." Queen Elitcal assured everyone that the battleships from the Real World had everything under control and encouraged everyone to enjoy their food and entertainment for her army would without a doubt finish off that ragged army in a matter of seconds.

Princess Meaira would not eat, nor would she move from the spot where she was for she had a perfect view overlooking the Real Sea and the battle that was taking place.

The ship from the Real World released a fearless attack, one that would surely finish off the subs for good. But Aqualeen ordered the three subs to dive further down in the Real Sea where the barrels would not be able to affect them.

When the smoke cleared, only the battleships from the Real Word and the capture ship that the men from The Golden Path were on could be seen. Princess Meaira began jumping up and down with joy as she assumed the battleships from the Real World had finally done it. She thought they had blown up the subs. "They are really gone," said Princess Meaira.

Queen Elitcal replied, "Yes they are. They are finally gone like I told you. Those subs are gone, but look to your right," said Queen Elitcal's guard, "There must be more than one hundred ships out there."

Queen Elitcal was furious when she found that what her guard said was true. Then she said to her Elite guards, "The battleships from the Real World will have to handle the situation on the Real Sea. We must focus on the battle that is taking place on land, for the army from The Golden Path are nothing without their men, so they must have a lot of weaknesses. It should be easy for us to finish them off with the skillful soldiers in both of our tribes armies.

"We will now launch a massive attack on this weak joke of an army from The Golden Path, and they will all pay for spoiling my perfect plan." Then Queen Elitcal looked at her Elite guards and asked them to find out where the unknown warship came from and why they were even involved in stopping the men from The Golden Path from being sold.

Queen Elitcal gave an order for the battleships from the Real World to disengage from battle and sail the capture ship with the men of The Golden Path on to the Real World without delay, because the oncoming attack from the unknown ships seemed to be too much for the Real World's battleships to handle. There were just way too many of the unknown enemies' ships since the others had arrived.

It had been a long night for all who were participating in the battle of the Real Sea, but now there was a renewed energy because of the presence of Czar Sharkaydo and his water fight fleet of warships, along with Queen Nstar and Dar-boo on board with him.

Queen Nstar noticed that a battleship from the Real World was towing the ship that was holding the men of The Golden Path captive. They were sailing at a furious pace toward the end of the Real Sea, which is the entrance to the Real World. Queen Nstar said to Czar Sharkaydo, "We must prevent them from reaching the Real World by any means necessary."

Queen Nstar and the Czar began to worry when they did not see any sign of the fighting subs that Aqualeen and the Title Holder women were on. Czar Sharkaydo told Queen Nstar he had already put out a finder keynote, and it had come back to him that the fleet of subs was fine.

Dar-boo said to Czar Sharkaydo, "If the battleships from the Real World realize they are outnumbered then they might try to sink the capture ship in order to escape the attack."

Czar Sharkaydo thanked Dar-boo for identifying the capture ship so they would not involve that ship in the attack.

Czar Sharkaydo immediately ordered his two generals, Der-nay and Kor-su, to attack all of the battleships from the Real World while his warship with Queen Nstar and Dar-boo would attack the battleship towing the capture boat the men from The Golden Path are on.

Then Czar Sharkaydo said to Dar-boo and Queen Nstar, "My ancestors built these warships. Let's see how well they really work." Then he put his warship in fighting mode.

Dar-boo noticed the warship lifted off the water as it started forward towards the Real World's ships. Czar Sharkaydo explained to Dar-boo how the warship performed. Czar Sharkaydo told Dar-boo and Queen Nstar, "The warship is a Hydro, meaning that in fighting mode it has jets to push it about thirty feet above the water. They move much faster than any battleship from the Real World."

"They were equipped with the best guns ever built for war," said Czar Sharkaydo Queen Nstar notices as they are flying over water that the ships from the Shark Tribe were quickly causing major damage to the Real World's fleet of battleships. Czar Sharkaydo ordered his fleet of ships to fire a massive attack.

Dar-boo looked up at the sky. The night was filled with fireworks from the battle of the Real Sea. Then Dar-boo noticed the battleship from the Real World, the *S. S. Rainier,* started releasing barrel bombs toward the capture ship. They were going to do away with the men from The Golden Path. Dar-boo asked Czar Sharkaydo, "Is there any way you can fire a round and change the course of the capture ship?" Czar Sharkaydo explained that if he missed and hit the capture ship it might sink.

Czar Sharkaydo released a fierce round at the battleship the *S.S. Rainier*, but the fleet from the Real World was defensively positioned. The Czar could not get to that side of the ship. Unbeknownst to the Czar they were protecting that side because it had already sustained heavy damage inflicted by the Women's fighting subs. The Czar explained to Queen Nstar and Dar-boo that they could finish off the enemy if only they had help on that side. At that point the Shark Tribe had already lost three warships to the battle of the Real Sea.

The battleships from the Real World came under heavy fire from Czar Sharkaydo and his fleet of warships, but the battleships from the Real World kept going forward toward the end of the Real Sea. "If they get to the end of the Real Sea there will be nothing more that can be done for the men of The Golden Path," said Czar Sharkaydo.

Both the *S.S. Rainier* and the capture ship were on fire by this time. Dar-boo said, "If we are going to have any chance of saving the men of The Golden Path we must act fast before it sinks into the Real Sea."

Czar Sharkaydo ordered his fleet of warships to stop firing on the *S.S. Rainier* and to instead concentrate and focus on destroying the rest of the ships from the Real World. Just then the Women's fighting subs appeared exactly in the position he had spoken of. They surrounded the ships that held the men of The Golden Path. Because the ships were on fire they had to act fast before the men of The Golden Path went down with their ships.

Aqualeen ordered Aliquel to take her warship, go beside the capture ship and help get the men of The Golden Path on board her ship. The other women would take care of the ship's guard. Aqualeen asked Nyrubi if she would like to order the command to sink the last battleships from the Real World. Nyrubi was honored to accept the request and ordered all guns from the subs to finish off the last seven ships from the Real World. They complied with the command and delivered a deadly blow to the fleets from the Real World .

The fleet of battleships from the Real World were finally defeated by the armies of the Shark Tribe along with the tribes of The Golden Path. They successfully rescued the men of The Golden Path from being taken away forever.

Nyrubi was holding little baby girl Olamae as she looked around and the only thing she saw was that the captive ship the men from The Golden Path were on was surrounded by the warships and fighting subs from the Shark Tribe, and it was a great sight to see. Sebnala was overcome with emotion as she looked at King Zhaun, Prince Amtar and all of the men being safely rescued and transferred to Aliquel's warship.

Aqualeen looked at Handfurya, Speed-Shay, Samikia, and Maysheara who were all standing together and asked them if they would like to fire the last round of gunfire to destroy and sink the capture ship into the Real Sea. Aqualeen told Handfurya to call out the command for the others to begin firing. Handfurya thanked Aqualeen for the great opportunity to be in charge. Aqualeen then asked the four young Title Holders their ages. They all answered her saying, "We are all about the same age."

"Which is?" Aqualeen asked.

Samikia replied, "We are seventeen years of age, Lady Aqualeen."

After all the men from The Golden Path were safely aboard Aliquel's warship, Handfurya yelled out the command, "Sink it!" The crew immediately fired on the enemy ship that had held the men captive just moments earlier. It was a direct hit, and down she went.

Everyone inside Aqualeen's subs began celebrating because the men of The Golden Path were finally out of danger.

Nyrubi said to her army, "Ladies, this is a great moment! We have successfully rescued our beloved men of The Golden Path from the grips of the enemy. I know that you would like nothing better than to see and hug your fathers, husbands, brothers, and friends, but we are not out of danger yet. There is still much that we have to do.. We must go and assist Moo-su and Keema along with the others from The Golden Path."

Aqualeen communicated to her husband Czar Sharkaydo for the first time since the Sea Lock gates had been opened. Aqualeen told Czar Sharkaydo that they needed to return to the shore to assist in the land battle. Czar Sharkaydo said to Aqualeen, "You go ahead and lead the way, and I will follow you."

Queen Nstar said to Aqualeen, "I do not have the words to let you know how truly grateful we are for your assistance. You risked your relationship with your husband and tribe as well as your very lives to help us. The truth is, were it not for your tribe the men from The Golden Path would never have been seen again. And without our men, our vulnerability would surely have made us victims to many schemes. Therefore you, the Shark Tribe, have literally saved our very existence."

Queen Nstar continued, "That incredible trust and confidence in each other is what makes your armies superior. The tribes of The Golden Path are just learning the importance of having Men's and Women's Armies. This day I am proud of all who live in the Land of the Seven for stepping up to the plate and delivering a successful campaign against an enemy that had us in an unfortunate position. Once again I thank you for introducing the tribes of The Golden Path to a whole new way of life and defense.

"Still, I must ask the Shark Tribe for two more favors. The first favor is for the Shark Tribe to take the Women's Army of The Golden Path to the shore in back of the Real Sea Palace. Moo-su along with Keema and the others are launching a massive land attack against the Elephant and Gorilla Tribes as we speak and need the assistance of the other women. We, the rest of the Women's Army from The Golden Path will join them. Our mission is not complete until the Elephant and Gorilla Tribes surrender to us, and I would love to see that moment," said Queen Nstar.

"The second favor I wish to ask of you is for the Shark Tribe to immediately take the men of The Golden Path to your tribe's territory and get them the medical attention and nourishment they need. They are too weak to assist the Women's Army in this final faze of the mission.

"So I ask you please Czar Sharkaydo, to indulge us by granting us these requests. We, the Women's Army of The Golden Path, will return to your tribe's territory after we complete our mission, which is to destroy everything about the Elephant and Gorilla Tribes."

Queen Nstar then said hello to Nyrubi for the first time since the Sea Lock gates were open, using the communicator box to the fighting sub Nyrubi to say, "It's been a long night."

Nyrubi replied, "A long night indeed, but a night that belongs to the Queens of the Land of the Seven which is all of us. Good job ladies!"

Then Nyrubi said to Queen Nstar, "I understand why you do not want the men to participate in this last battle against the Elephant and Gorilla Tribe. I am fully prepared for all the women to show our men we can finish a mission just as well as they would, and I would like to thank Shar-nu's uncle, Czar Sharkaydo, for allowing us the privilege of getting to know the Shark Tribe. I am truly grateful for that."

The fighting fleet of warships and subs from the Shark Tribe took the Women's Army to the shore in back of the Sea Palace in the Elephant Tribe's territory. Moo-su and Keema's land armies had already begun a fierce attack against their opposition. The men from The Golden Path stayed on board the Shark Tribe's warship to be taken back with the Shark Tribe and recover from their ordeal.

All of the Women's Armies came together back on land and they began hugging each other with joy and happiness for what they had just accomplished on the Real Sea waters; however, Dar-boo quickly put a stop to their celebration. He said to the women warriors, "I know you all are tired and you just want to be alone with the men of The Golden Path, but they are no good to us right now. I must ask all of you women to put aside all of your hurts and your feelings around missing your loved ones, to press forward through this last attack against the Elephant and Gorilla Tribes. You truly have done everything asked of you and more, but you are still needed. We must complete our objective of this mission. So I am asking all of the Women's Armies to rise up one more time for The Golden Path. Furthermore, I would like to take this time to thank each of you for coming together when you really did not have to.

"We have learned a lot about each other. We have learned that no matter what tribe you come from, women can come together as one and become a massive force to be reckoned with.

"I also would like to welcome our new members of The Golden Path, Tozara and the 49er Women. They also did not have to be here with us, but they gave their all. We, the tribes of The Golden Path, appreciate and welcome you Tozara."

Tozara walked up to Dar-boo and told him it was not hard to see the determination in the faces of the Women's Army. "I was impressed by the way the Title Holder women look out for each other no matter who you are. I must say I am glad the 49er Women had the opportunity to get to know the Women's Army of The Golden Path as well as the Shark Tribe.

"The 49er Women are honored to fight alongside your Women's Army. I would like to tell Shar-nu that her courage helped me to know myself and believe in myself a lot more. I hope we can become good friends. I would like to volunteer at the Tree Patch whenever you need."

Shar-nu thanked Tozara and the 49er Women. Then Shar-nu asked if every woman would bow her head to give their fallen soldier, Teela, seven seconds. Everyone bowed their heads and said together, "We love you and we will miss you Teela," as Speed-Shay held baby girl Olamae.

Queen Nstar asked if there was anyone else that had something they wanted to say. No one spoke up and so Queen Nstar gave final instructions for the impending battle. She said, "We will now go and assist Moo-su, Keema and the others. We must stay focused on the matter of defeating our enemy and that means that whatever Moo-su asks of us, we must do without hesitation. Moo-su has a plan and we must trust and follow her orders to the letter if we are to be victorious."

Queen Nstar then asked the women, "Are you ready?"

"Yes!" said the army as they started going up the Real Sea Mountains towards the Sea Palace and Queen Elitcal and Princess Meaira.

As Queen Nstar, Nyrubi and Dar-boo approached the palace walls, Moo-su, Keema, and the Council Armies were just inside the palace gates. They were wearing down their enemy. The Elephant Tribe and the Gorilla Tribe were on their last line of defense in an effort to stop the rain of attacks coming their way. Moo-su felt it could be over if they were to receive some assistance in this final push. Just as Keema told Moo-su they might have to continue holding outside the palace until the next day, Keema and Moo-su witnessed a sight of joy. It was the other members of her Women's Army from The Golden Path. Queen Nstar as well as Nyrubi walked over to Moo-su and asked her what she needed them to do. Moo-su told Nyrubi and Queen Nstar, "Alert the women troops, for we are going into the Queen of the Elephant Tribe's quarters tonight to capture both Queen Elitcal and Princess Meaira."

Keema told the other Title Holder women, "I was just thinking about camping out for the night, but since you all have arrived I believe it would be wise to attack now." At that very moment a long explosion went off. It was the Wild Boar Tribe battling forward toward the main quarter of the palace where they believed the Queen of the Elephant Tribe was secured.

They had finally broken through to the palace and were nearing the Queen of the Elephant Tribe's quarters. Meanwhile inside of Queen Elitcal's quarters, her royal guards were pleading with her to abandon her plan and escape through the secret tunnel while they still had a chance. Queen Elitcal refused, saying to her guards and Princess Meaira, "No, I sincerely believed it would not come to this; however, because of the surprise battle on the Real Sea my Plan A was clearly soiled by the enemy. However, as your Queen and a Master Planner, you would do well not to underestimate me. The unwritten creed of a Master Planner is to plan for the best but always prepare for the worst. Well, my fellow tribesmen we have indeed come to 'the worst.'

"This is plan B, previously prepared just in case we had to abort our mission and flee. This plan gives me the opportunity to speak and look directly at the tribes of The Golden Path without them ever getting the chance to capture me or Princess Meaira. I already have it set up whereby one push of a button brings forth a mirror. Inside that mirror my exact image will suddenly appear right before their eyes. This catches them totally off guard and while they are completely mystified my image says to them everything that I want them to hear. This diversion gives us plenty of time to escape through the secret tunnels and return to the Real World.

"Plan C is to get settled and connected again in the Real World and then organize yet another army to go up against the tribes of The Golden Path. My next plan will not fail. We will be ready to fight by land, sea, and air if need be. You are welcome to go with me if you'd like Princess Meaira."

One of Queen Elitcal's generals begged her, yet again, to leave. They could all plainly hear that the Women's Army of The Golden Path was just outside of the Queen's quarters. That meant that they had already come through many treacherous barriers and dangerous traps to reach the fortified, ten-inch thick, ivory doors at the entryway. The General said to the Queen, "My Lady, that gate will not hold them off much longer."

Queen Elitcal refused to abandon her Plan B. Plan B called for her to stand right where she was to let the Women's Army get a good look at who had thought of such an elaborate and strategic plan. A plan that had rendered the tribes of The Golden Path so vulnerable and helpless. She was sure, however, that she had helped them in some strange way for they somehow survived her plan to get rid of all the men of The Golden Path forever.

Princess Meaira asked Queen Elitcal, "How are we going to be able to go through the time lock to get to the Real world without aging and growing old?"

Queen Elitcal told Princess Meaira that she still had in her possession, the time shell she used to travel back and forth while attending college in the Real World. "I saved them for later use. No one from The Golden Path can go through or enter the time lock for they are already too old to survive the aging process it puts you through. That is why I would like them to see me, and I would like to see Dar-boo the so called Peace Keeper, Queen Nstar, Nyrubi and the Council of The Golden Path. I want them never to forget me. I will promise them I will return for another chance to take over The Golden Path and rule all of The Land of Seven. The people all over the Land of the Seven parallel to earth will bow to me, Queen Elitcal, or they shall die."

The Wild Boar Tribe along with Nyrubi's troops were the first to enter the Queen's quarters. When all of the members of The Golden Path along with the 49er Women finally entered the Queen's palace they came face to face with the image in the mirror of Queen Elitcal.

Queen Elitcal's first words to the tribe of The Golden Path were, "Congratulations are in order for the tribes of The Golden Path. Once again you have soiled an attempt by the Elephant Tribe, along with the Gorilla Tribe and Game Hunters, to destroy and capture the land of The Golden Path and rule it for ourselves as we see fit.

"I am Queen Elitcal of the Elephant Tribe. I am also the Plan Master of this effort to attack the tribes of The Golden Path at your most vulnerable points, which should have been the sky and the sea, since none of your tribes have ever experienced attacks from either of these places. I quickly surmised that those two places were your weak points and where we could do the most damage to you. But somehow you all managed to survive both of my massive plans to take over The Golden Path. I will say this to you, my plans would have worked perfectly had it not been for the Women's Armies and the unknown tribe, both of which I had no knowledge. Nevertheless, I still have one more plan up my sleeve, but first I must return to the Real World. I know some of you are asking yourself , 'How could that be?' I have my ways. Some of you from The Golden Path might get an idea to stop this little jaunt to the Real World, however, you might want to think about that a little bit further before entering the time locks. All of you are too old to go through the time lock. I will go to the Real World to form a massive military force, one that will crush all of the tribes from the Land of the Seven, by sea, land, and sky. There will not be any survivors. Neither men nor women will be spared, and it will happen when you least expect it."

Dar-boo stepped in front of everyone from The Golden Path and said to Queen Elitcal, "Do not think we will not come after you. You are sadly mistaken if you think no one from The Golden Path can procure a time journey shield. We, the tribes of The Golden Path, will find a way to defeat you once again. We'll be right behind you, Queen Elitcal, whenever you make a move. And we, the tribes of The Golden Path and the Land of the Seven, will be waiting with a well-trained military force capable of battling by land, sky, or water. Both genders will learn how to defend the Land of the Seven and The Golden Path. You are a great Plan Master, but we have many new up and coming Plan Masters ourselves, including myself. I'm sure we can sit down and think up a master plan that would go through the time lock with a shield and stop you from forming any kind of army. Do not be too confident."

Queen Elitcal along with Princess Meaira began to laugh at Dar-boo and his foolish statements. "Fool, you cannot think that the tribes of The Golden Path will always be able to defeat us."

Princess Meaira appeared in the mirror as she began to speak to Queen Nstar, "I will not stop until I see you pay for the death of my father. Do not get comfortable, because that will be the precise time when Queen Elitcal and I return to finish off the tribes of The Golden Path. I must say this to the Women's Army of The Golden Path: you've done well in defending your land and freeing your men from the capture ship. That was a great occasion for everyone. One you should remember. For it will not be long before Queen Elitcal and I, Princess Meaira return for our prize, which is The Golden Path."

"Until we meet again Dar-boo and tribes of The Golden Path. It will not be long before your happiness is shattered by attacks from the sky, land, and water. I will see all of you in the future," said Queen Elitcal.

Queen Nstar told Queen Elitcal, "If ever your two tribes had a chance to defeat the tribes from The Golden Path along with the Shar Tribe it was now, in your latest plan against us.

"When you return to the Land of the Seven we will all be waiting for you and our military will be even more forceful, more skillful, quicker in attack and able to defeat our enemies with fewer casualties."

The images of Queen Elitcal and Princess Meaira in the mirror began to disappear as Queen Elitcal said to Dar-boo, "You should be very proud of the leader of the Women's Army, for without her my plan would surely have been successful."

Dar-boo looked at Moo-su and said, "You have made yourself into a great leader."

Nyrubi walked up to where Moo-su, Queen Nstar and Dar-boo were standing and said, "Are we just going to let them walk away ? They need to pay for what they have done! They need to pay for all the damage they have done to our land and to our people, I cannot believe we are just going to let them walk away."

Keema walked over to Nyrubi and gave her a hug. "We have won. We finally won and don't anyone forget that!"

Prince Donshu said, "Keema is right. We won an important war against the Elephant and Gorilla Tribes along with the Game Hunters. Both the men and the women of The Golden Path have a great deal to be proud of, for this was a war which tested all of the Land of Seven, not just the tribes, villages and towns of The Golden Path. We should be enjoying the victory we just won.

"Moo-su you led a newly formed army, a Woman's Army. You went up against all the odds and won!" said Prince Donshu, speaking to the Women's Army of The Golden Path as well as the 49er Women.

"Moo-su," Dar-boo said to her, "on the journey in which you have led us we met some powerful allies who have the same values and common beliefs.

"So I would like to take this time to thank each and every one of you who risked your life to assist The Golden Path. 49er Women for their expertise in battle which helped us defeat the Elephant and Gorilla Tribe. We are truly grateful and look forward to you becoming members of The Golden Path. Valley Diggers, Dark Rangers, Village of Michelgray, Town of Cottenberg, Town of Tree Patch and once again, the newly discovered Shark Tribe we of The Golden Path will never forget your loyalty, your courage and your fierce fighting skills. You came to assist us without even being asked. You have proven to be true allies and we The Golden Path will always be there for you, should you ever need anything.

"We also need to handle some unfinished business," Dar-boo told everyone. "The Council must vote on two matters: the Wild Boar Tribe receiving their land and the 49er Women becoming members of The Golden Path."

Then the members of the Council took Dar-boo to the side and said to him, "Dar-boo, both of these matters are very important, however, the men of The Golden Path are not here. This business should be addressed once we are all together. It is an issue of respect."

Dar-boo said to the Council, "I stand corrected. You are right."

Dar-boo then went back in front of the women and apologized for his over- zealousness. He went on to reiterated The Council's decision to postpone the vote in accordance with Golden Path tradition to have all of the Title Holders present, not just the women.

All the members of The Golden Path said, "Here, Here."

Then Samikia walked over to Dar-boo and said, "The young Plan Master has an idea."

"Who might that be?" replied Dar-boo.

Samikia said, "It is Handfurya."

"Handfurya wishes to speak with me about a plan? Come, come forward Handfurya, let's hear this plan of yours."

Handfurya told Dar-boo, "The Queen of the Elephant Tribe spoke about the members of The Golden Path being too old to go through the locks to the Real Word, but if we sent Olamae and my little sister Farshell who is now seven years of age to journey through the time locks it would make her fifteen years of age and baby girl Olamae would be eight years of age. They could get through the time locks and put a stop to Queen Elitcal's diabolical plans with no time limitations. They are absolutely capable of carrying out this mission. We the people of the Land of the Seven are superior beings so in the Real World these young women will possess immortal power and they will have a huge advantage. All we have to do is teach Farshell what she and Olamae need to do in order to have a successful mission."

Dar-boo told Handfurya, "We the members of The Golden Path will decide on your plan and get back to you with our decision. You have done well Handfurya."

Handfurya told Dar-boo, "If we are going to send the two baby Title Holders through the time locks we have to do it soon."

Moo-su addressed her Women's Army of The Golden Path, the 49er Women, the Council Army and the Wild Boar Tribe's Army. "Our mission is now complete and we are done here. I would say it is safe to say victory is ours, and we can finally be with our beloved men of The Golden Path, whom we are missing dearly. We can now go to them and let them know how important they are to us and The Golden Path. Also, we need to let the men know that we too were fooled and went into the Real Sea Mountains thinking it was another cave in the mountain. Since none of us was familiar with the terrain there was no way to know that what we saw was not real. It was indeed a beautiful plan, we were all duped. Therefore, we must assure our men that they have nothing to be ashamed of. Now, lets go and celebrate with all of the great men from The Golden Path and relax. We deserve it."

"Well said, Moo-su," replied Prince Donshu, as both began their journey towards the Shark Tribe's territory where the men of The Golden Path were waiting for their return.

As the victorious armies of the Wild Boar Tribe, Councils and the Women's Army along with the 49er Women came over the last hill before the Shark Tribe Territory near Cameleeta Beach, they were greeted by a hero's parade. They made their way toward Czar Sharkaydo anxiously, knowing that the Title Holder men of The Golden Path would also be waiting for them with open arms.

It had been a long time since the men and the women from The Golden Path had gotten the chance to spend time with each other. This would be a great welcome home celebration for everyone who lived in the Land of the Seven. This had been a victory of great magnitude, especially considering that they had no prior training with each other. They fought as true warriors in battle.

The people of the Shark Tribe along with the people from the town of Cottonberg, the Village of Michelgrey, the town of Darnell, the children from the Tree Patch where Shar-nu was from, The Three Streets, Deer, Buffalo, and Gazelle Streets, were all present at the parade.

Moo-su and the others turned the corner to the Czar's palace which was literally packed with well wishers, and then they saw them. The men of The Golden Path. Oh they looked so wonderful. It had been so long since they had seen their loved ones. Speed-Shay saw her father Prince Amtar on the steps beside Emperor Albertine. Speed-Shay began running toward her father and he in turn began running to her. Prince Amtar also saw his wife Graceshell who is Speed-Shay's mother and called out to her.

All of a sudden everyone broke formation and the women and the men ran toward each other.

Samikia rushed over to her brother, Sergeant Carlay of the Salmon Tribe. Handfurya was being hugged and held by her father, Chancellor Shenot of the Hyena Tribe. Maysheara was already with her father, Prince Donshu of the Wild Boar Tribe. They stood holding each other and watching the others.

Sebnala hugged her husband, Leo-Paul, and her uncle, King Zhaun of the Lion Tribe. Suddenly King Zhaun was surrounded and was being hugged by his two daughters, Nyrubi and Shar-nu.

Moo-su was actually lifted up into the air by her son, Afro-Light, from the Jaguar Tribe. He was so very happy to see his mother! Nyrubi called out to her husband, Afro-Light, as they ran toward each other.

Queen Nstar was watching with joy and excitement as all of her members of The Golden Path united, rejoicing as one. Just then a man stuck his hand out in front of her and said, "My Queen Nstar, may I have this dance with you?"

Queen Nstar looked up to see none other than Dar-boo, the Peace Keeper from the Deer Tribe. Queen Nstar said to Dar-boo, "Why, sir, you certainly may. I would be honored."

As they started to dance together someone said, "How are you two going to dance without any music?" It was O'Hally, originally from the Tiger Tribe and now from The Three Streets of The Golden Path. O'Hally opened his arms to his sister Queen Nstar.

Dar-boo said to Queen Nstar, "It's OK, Queen. That's your brother, and you two need to talk."

Queen Nstar agreed to talk to her brother O'Hally, but only if Dar -boo came with her. Dar-boo told Queen Nstar he would be honored to be asked to accompany her.

Emperor Albertine along with his son, Waterflow, walked over to Samikia and said, "You have done very well for yourself young lady, very well indeed. I, the Emperor of the Salmon Tribe, am very honored by your participation in the Women's Army."

Waterflow looked at Samikia and said to her, "I knew you and the other Title Holder women, along with your army, could come free us."

Samikia hugged Waterflow and told him she was happy to see him again. Waterflow replied, "I've missed you a great deal also, Samikia."

Keema and Brighthea were in awe when they first saw Chief Grawn of the Bear Tribe. He had lost seventy pounds. Chief Grawn asked his wife Brighthea if she liked his new look. Brighthea walked up to her husband, Chief Grawn, and said to him, "I love it when you are big, when you are small. I love you whether you are little or big. I just love you, Chief Grawn of the Bear Tribe."

When everyone was finished welcoming each other home, King Zhaun of the Lion Tribe walked over to Moo-su and asked her to marry him right there and then. Everyone around was shocked and in awe that these two great leaders had fallen for each other. Shar-nu asked her sister Nyrubi if she knew about the two of them already. Nyrubi replied, "No, I did not know. Did you?" Nyrubi asked her husband Afro-Light.

Afro-Light said that he knew nothing about them, but he was glad for the two of them as Afro-Light's mother Moo-su answered, "Yes!" to King Zhaun's request for her hand in marriage.

Czar Sharkaydo welcomed all of the members of The Golden Path to the Shark Tribe's Territory. "We are truly allies in the survival of the Land of the Seven and of The Golden Path."

Dar-boo and the Council of The Golden Path said to all of the members, "Before we go to celebrate this glorious occasion of marriage between two great people who I love very much, we still have some unfinished business to deal with."

King Zhaun and Chief Grawn simultaneously said, "What unfinished business?"

"The business is this," said Dar-boo. "We are very sorry to have to tell you this Chancellor Shenot of the Hyena Tribe, but your little daughter has been chosen to journey through the time lock to the Real World in order to put a stop to Queen Elitcal of the Elephant Tribe's plan. She plans to go to the Real World to form an army and come back to the Land of the Seven to destroy us."

Chancellor Shenot yelled, "No, not my baby girl, Farshell!"

Dar-boo said, "She is needed to look after little baby girl Olamae while they both go do the task of stopping Queen Elitcal."

The Council said to Chancellor Shenot and every member of The Golden Path, "We know we all should have had the chance to vote on the matter of Farshell and baby girl Olamae, however, we thought it should be done right away while the time lock gate was still open. So we went ahead and made the decision. Both Dar-boo and the members of the Council will have to live with our decision for the rest of our lives, but when the new Plan Master of The Golden Path, Handfurya told us the plan and we went over it again and again it seemed the right thing to do."

Chancellor Shenot fell to his knees and said, "Good-bye my little Queen Farshell. I will always miss you."

Handfurya rushed over to her father, Chancellor Shenot along with many other Title Holders from The Golden Path.

Then King Zhaun of the Lion Tribe said to the Council and Dar-boo , "Who is this little baby you speak of named Olamae?" Dar-boo said to King Zhaun, "Olamae is your niece; Teela's baby girl. She had this baby while returning from the Women's Army's first mission."

King Zhaun asked Dar-boo, "Where is Teela right now?"

Dar-boo said to King Zhaun, "Teela died saving my life from an arrow coming my way."

King Zhaun said, "Teela died? You mean Teela is no longer with us?"

Sebnala said to her uncle, King Zhaun, "Do not feel bad. She gave her life to save Dar-boo, the Peace Keeper of the Deer Tribe, and now her daughter is giving her life to save the Land of the Seven and The Golden Path. So, Uncle please do not feel bad."

King Zhaun thanked his niece Sebnala then walked up to Czar Sharkaydo. "I am King Zhaun of the Lion Tribe, I would like to take this opportunity to thank you for all of the help you gave the members of The Golden Path in freeing us men from the captive ship we were on."

"I am Czar Sharkaydo of the Shark Tribe, and I did what I know you would have done if I needed help. You are welcome, King Zhaun"

Prince Amtar, along with Prince Donshu said, "'We have a lot to be thankful for, so let's begin by celebrating King Zhaun and Moo-su's marriage and wishing Farshell and Olamae safety, as they travel to the Real World through the Time Locks."

Everyone from The Golden Path and the Land of the Seven said, "Here, here!"

# Tribes and Tributes

Tribes of The Golden Path honor the following ethnic groups and the endurance of their cultures despite great hardships, some of which are indicated below.

| | |
|---|---|
| Jaguar | Black Americans (Slavery) |
| Cheetah | African Tribes |
| Hyena | Hispanics (California) |
| Lion | Native Americans (Trail of Tears) |
| Salmon | Jewish Peoples (Holocaust) |
| Bear | Chinese (Railroad Builders) |
| Shark | Polish Warsaw (Fought Nazis by themselves) |
| Tiger | Irish Immigrants |
| Elephant | The Romans |
| Gorilla | The Greeks |

# ABOUT THE AUTHOR

Eric the First lives and writes in Seattle, WA. This is his first novel. He is currently working on his second book, entitled *Slave Heaven*.

LaVergne, TN USA
04 December 2010
207369LV00003B/2/P